LIGHTHOUSE
THREADS

LIGHTHOUSE THREADS

A Virginia Davies Quilt Mystery
Book Ten

By
David Ciambrone

RISING PHOENIX PRESS ®

Text Copyright © 2024 David Ciambrone

All rights reserved.
Published 2024 by Progressive Rising Phoenix Press, LLC
www.progressiverisingphoenix.com

ISBN: 978-1-958640-68-5

Printed in the U.S.A.

Back Cover Photo "Lots of Gold Coin in Treasure Sack at Black Background." Stock Photo ID: 1508771672, By hichaa. Image used under license from ShutterStock.com.

Book and Cover design by William Speir
Visit: http://www.williamspeir.com

ACKNOWLEDGMENTS

Writing is a solitary affair, but, any author will also tell you their writing depends on a host of others who have provided needed information, ideas, inspiration, critiques, just plain support when we needed it, and someone to listen when things go awry. To this end, I'd like to thank the following people and groups for their support in bringing this book to life:

My great publisher Amanda M. Thrasher and editors at Progressive Rising Phoenix Press, LLC. Without them, this book would not have seen the light of day.

The San Gabriel Writer's League mystery critique group.

My late wife Kathy for her inspiration and support and the quilt used in the story and on the cover.

PROLOGUE

October 1923—Somewhere along the southern shore of Lake Ontario

On a cold, overcast, and foggy night, the deck squeaked as six men quietly struggled with a large, locked trunk containing a half million dollars in gold coins, weighing a little over a thousand pounds, and secured it into the lifeboat of the lake schooner Midnight.

"We need to hurry," a bearded man said. "A customs boat comes this way every few days. I want to be out of here if it shows up. They'd love to catch us with all that booze in the hold and all this gold."

"I agree." Another one of the men glanced around. "Everyone else is below deck now, but the watch will be up shortly. I don't want to think about what they would do to us if they caught us. Let's move faster."

The men paused to tug their coats tighter, then carefully swung the lifeboat over the water. Climbing into it, the men lowered the boat into the frigid gray waters of Lake Ontario. It settled into the lake with barely a splash. The two biggest men rowed the boat toward shore, two hundred yards away, and into a small, tree-lined cove. There they ran it up on the rocky beach. Fog swirled through the broadleaf forest of mainly maple, oak, and birchbark trees. Manhandling the trunk, they struggled as they hauled it up a slight slope to level ground and a waiting panel truck. They stopped to catch their breath. Glancing back to see if they were being followed, they then drove six miles to an abandoned stone lighthouse and pulled up next to a rundown garage near it. They opened the rickety doors, pulled the truck inside, and parked. They swung the squeaking, large wooden doors closed, locked them and stepped back on the gravel driveway.

One of the men looked up at the cloud-filled sky, then listened. "Hey, mates, something's amiss around here."

"No one followed us." The shortest man looked around. "I don't see or hear anything except the sound of the waves on the beach below."

"That's just it. No bug noises. No crickets or other insects chirping. Nothing. It's too quiet."

"Maybe it's because of the storm that's coming or the dampness of the fog, or because it's night. Let's get the hell out of here." The shortest man shivered as a breeze swept through the trees. He jumped as an owl hooted from a nearby tree. "This place gives me the willies."

As they walked to their car hidden around the side of the garage, a vehicle's headlights flashed on from a clearing near the empty and dilapidated lighthouse keeper's home, blinding them. In the illumination, the men froze. A machine gun roared from next to the vehicle for a few seconds. The shooter watched as the men convulsed from the multiple bullets slamming into them and fell into the dirt and weeds next to the garage door.

After the gunfire stopped, a man stepped into the car's lights, holding a Thompson machine gun, and watched the dead men for a minute. The machine gunner then opened the trunk of the car and removed a five gallon can of gasoline. He splashed the contents on and into the car and tossed a lit cigarette lighter in. The car burst into flames. Fire and smoke billowed toward the clouded sky. He casually retrieved the keys of the truck from one of the dead men and entered the garage. He opened the back of the truck, unlocked the trunk with a key from his pocket, and removed a single gold coin. He strolled back to the dead men and tossed the coin on one of them. Then he returned to the garage and drove the truck—with the coins—into the damp, foggy night.

A short Seneca Indian woman watched from the top of the lighthouse.

CHAPTER 1

Present Day—Coast of Lake Ontario along New York State

Virginia Davies Clark adjusted her blonde ponytail protruding from the rear of her red baseball cap, settled back into her seat, and drove the rented, silver Honda Pilot at the speed limit along the coast road with the lake on her left and a few houses nestled in the forest on her right. She glanced at her friend Natalie sitting next to her.

Natalie North, a knitter and new quilter, glanced out the side window. "I love the trees. The scenery is beautiful and all… nothing like home in Texas. How long until we get there?"

Virginia glanced at the navigation system's display. "About a half hour. What's the hurry? It's June, we're on vacation, going to a quilt retreat."

Natalie pushed her sunglasses up on top of her blonde hair, adjusted her five-foot frame in her seat, and sighed. "We'd be there by now if I were driving."

Virginia laughed. "We'd be either in jail or dead. You like to drive at warp speed. The local cops frown on driving close to the speed of light."

"Party pooper."

"You haven't finished your running narrative from that guidebook on the area and the lodge we're going to yet. At this safe speed, you will have time to finish."

Natalie set the open book on her legs. "I already told you about the history of the old lighthouse and the Inn. The history of the area goes way back before the American Revolution. The lighthouse and this section of the Lake Ontario coast was an active pirate area in the 1600s, and because of the numerous coves, it was popular with smugglers and bootleggers during prohibition."

"Interesting. Anything else we should know?"

"The new owners converted the Inn into a conference center and retreat venue a few years ago. Now it's big with the quilters, crafts people, and businesses around here." Natalie studied the book and swallowed. "Oh, boy."

Virginia turned to her and frowned. "Oh, boy, what?"

"Nothing."

"Natalie North if you don't tell me what 'oh, boy' meant, I'll pull over and read it myself."

"Okay. But remember what I just said, you promised your husband you would behave yourself and not find any dead bodies to investigate."

"Who said anything about dead bodies? We're here for a quilting retreat and to have fun. Now, about the 'oh, boy.' Did someone die and now his ghost has taken up residence?"

Natalie shook her head. "No. Well... okay, according to the history of the lighthouse and Inn, it supposedly still houses a huge chest of gold stolen from a smuggler and bootlegger back in the 1920s. The guidebook says six men were murdered after they stole the gold off a lake schooner suspected of being a smuggling ship. The killer was never apprehended, and the gold was never recovered."

"Stolen gold, murders?" Virginia's face brightened. "We need to find the gold."

"You promised your husband, Andy, no more turning up dead bodies on your vacations."

Virginia turned, "How much gold?"

Natalie picked up the book, flipped a few pages, then answered, "Half a million dollars in gold coins from 1923. That's a half million in 1923 dollars."

"What's that in today's dollars?"

"I don't know. But let's do some calculating." Natalie used her cellphone for the Internet then fished a notebook, pen, and a calculator out of her black leather backpack. She did some quick math. "Okay, according to the Internet the coins were probably $20 gold pieces. There were a few different kinds, but since we don't know which ones were stolen, I used the average. For half a million dollars that would mean they had 25,000 gold coins, give or take a few."

Virginia slowed for a blind curve, then accelerated. "That's a hell of a lot of gold coins."

"Yes, and today each coin is worth about $2,400. Therefore 25,000 times 2400 equals..." Natalie fingered her calculator. "About sixty million dollars or so."

"That's a lot of millions. This will be quite a challenge."

"It's been missing since 1923, and you think we can find it while at a quilt retreat for a week?"

Virginia glanced at the navigation system screen. "We're almost there. We've solved cases in that amount of time before."

"Okay, I'll give you that. But remember, we are on vacation in a scenic area at a quilt retreat." Natalie waved her arm at the scenery flashing by. "Look… beautiful broadleaf trees, maples, oaks, birch, nice green fields, a stream with fish in it. And we can look forward to sewing, quilting, nature hikes, swimming, sailing, eating, and drinking being our prime objectives. Treasure hunting is not on the list."

"How'd you know there were fish in that stream?"

Natalie gave Virginia a guilty look. "A trout jumped when I glanced at the water. So, we agree, sewing, quilting, eating, drinking, and time in the Jacuzzi, assuming they have one. You did bring your bikini, didn't you?"

"Yes. The red one. And we can do some treasure hunting, which may include a few hikes," Virginia said.

Natalie shook her head. "Remember what you promised your husband. No dead bodies."

"You said that already. Besides, dead bodies aren't on my to do list."

"I also promised my dear boyfriend, Jeff, we'd keep out of trouble and away from dead bodies. But everywhere you and I go, and even at home, we have a knack for turning up corpses. My promise may be a little hard to keep. Do the local police know we're coming?"

Virginia stuck her tongue out at Natalie. "No, the police don't know we're coming." She slowed and turned down a dense, shaded, tree-lined gravel road toward Lake Ontario. Pebbles pinged the undercarriage of the car as they made their way down the road under a canopy of hefty branches. They emerged into a large gravel parking lot that overlooked the lake in front of them. On the right was a three-story, log-constructed building with a red metal roof. A large covered porch with massive wooden posts swept around the structure. A dozen cars were parked in the lot. A white wooden fence ran along the edge of the parking lot, and along the drop-off to the lake and beach below. An opening for a set of stairs was in the middle of the fence. Virginia spied a similar set in a grassy area near the lodge.

Virginia parked near the fence that bordered the grass in front of the lodge. "Well, we're here. Isn't it great? Looks like something you'd see in the Adirondacks."

"Virginia, you are *in* the Adirondacks. At least I think we're in the Adirondacks. Catskills maybe? You've been to this part of the country before, so this should not be new to you." Natalie grabbed her backpack and climbed out of the car. She stepped to the rear of the vehicle and glanced at Virginia sliding out of the front seat. "Let's get our bags and go register. Then we can explore." Natalie pointed up a hill behind the Inn. "That must be the old lighthouse that is mentioned in the guidebook."

"I think you're right." Water gently lapped the pebble beach. The pungent tang of wood smoke hung in the air as Virginia pulled her two suitcases and her backpack from the vehicle's trunk.

Natalie removed her suitcases, closed the trunk, and gazed around at the view. "Beautiful. Doesn't look like a place that would have secrets."

After checking in, finding their suite, and unpacking, Virginia closed the dresser drawer, turned, and re-entered the closet. She examined the three hooks on the side of the wall and the two bars for hanging clothes. She backed out and shut the door, almost running into Natalie.

Natalie frowned. "What are you doing?"

"Trying to see if there was a hidden door to a secret passage."

Natalie raised an eyebrow. "Find anything?"

"No. But if this place is as old as the guidebook says, I bet there is a secret passage. In these parts, old buildings sometimes had them."

"They've renovated the place a few times since the 1920s. I'm sure if there were any passages, the owners knew about them and probably closed them or used them for entertaining the guests. This section isn't that old, so it probably doesn't have any secret passages."

Virginia shrugged. "Probably right." She stepped to the window and looked out at the cove and Lake Ontario from their second-floor suite. "God, that's big. And it's freshwater. It looks like an ocean. It still takes my breath away every time I see it."

"Yeah, and it isn't the biggest." Natalie plopped onto the bed and looked at Virginia. "From what I remember being told when I was an actress and did a movie on this lake up near the Thousand Islands, the great lakes can generate their own weather at times. You don't want to be out there in a boat when the lake decides to get uppity." She popped a grape in her mouth.

"You're right. I made that mistake once. Once was enough. Where did you get the grape?"

"From the fruit basket in the living room. It's from the woman who invited us to this retreat." Natalie smiled. "Nice that you booked us a suite."

"The basket was thoughtful, and I like us being together. Makes things easier." Virginia looked at the clock on the bedstand. "Three o'clock. Let's grab some of the fruit and maybe take a stroll down by the water before we get ready for dinner."

After returning from their walk and showering, Virginia finished combing her hair and applied some lipstick in the bathroom. She straightened her dark-blue blouse and her jeans, then entered the living room area. Natalie, who people said looked like Bernadette from the TV show *The Big Bang*

Theory, was sitting on the small couch wearing a tight red blouse—straining to contain her 38D breasts—and black slacks. Natalie was reading the guidebook from the car.

Virginia smiled, "Did you finish unpacking?"

Natalie nodded. "Yes."

"You ready to go eat?"

"I'm always ready for that." Natalie held up the guidebook. "You know this story about the smugglers and the lost treasure is intriguing. Six men were murdered the night the treasure was stolen. Maybe I'll help you find it."

Virginia beamed. "Great. We make a hell of a detective team."

"The treasure is supposed to be around here," Natalie said.

"It's been here for what… a hundred years?" asked Virginia. "And no one has found it yet."

Natalie closed the guidebook. "From what the book says, it may have been moved to who-knows-where."

Virginia shrugged her shoulder. "When have we not found what we were looking for?"

Natalie grinned. "I'll help and try to find it. I may even be able to keep you from turning up more fresh dead bodies. But that usually doesn't work." Natalie rose and tossed the book on the coffee table then hurried across the room toward the door. "Coming? Dinner awaits."

Virginia joined her at the door. "This is going to be fun… and look how pretty it is around here. The quilting and sewing will be great without distractions."

Natalie wrinkled her brow. "Virginia, there are sixty million distractions, but for now, let's go meet the others here, have dinner, and enjoy the evening."

They walked into the dining room, which looked like a pine wood-paneled space the size of a ballroom. Running down the center of the room was a large, heavy, polished-oak table that could seat fifteen. They noticed twelve people milling around, some holding drinks.

Natalie leaned close to Virginia and whispered, "There are three men in the group, and if the women's eyes could shoot real daggers, we'd be dead."

"The men seem to approve of us."

"Of course they do. We're about half the age of the other ladies and look sexy. And, Virginia, your blouse doesn't hide your ample assets very well, either. To the chagrin of the other women, we have suddenly become the center of the men's attentions."

Before Natalie could say anything more, Virginia charged toward the small group of men.

"Oh, boy, we're off to a good start," mumbled Natalie. She shook her head and started after Virginia.

A tall athletic looking man with black hair and green eyes, dressed in a blue sport shirt and jeans, lowered his drink as Virginia and Natalie strutted up to the group of men. He glanced up and down at the two women approaching, then smiled. "Good evening, ladies. May I get you any drinks?"

Natalie grinned. "I'd like a strawberry daiquiri."

He looked at Virginia. "And you miss?"

"A piña colada would be nice," Virginia purred.

The other two men quickly moved closer and started to ask questions and discuss the quilt retreat.

Virginia mumbled to Natalie, "The quilting and treasure hunting will be easy compared to handling these three."

"I agree. The guy getting us drinks could be a problem. I think he's already undressed us multiple times in his head."

Virginia sighed. "That's okay, but we'll have to keep his hands occupied sewing."

"Can I just drug him for the duration?"

"With what? Wait, don't answer that. You said you'd try and prevent me from turning up dead bodies. Do I have to prevent you from creating them for me?"

The two men standing near them looked puzzled about what was just said.

Natalie smiled as the tall man returned with their drinks.

CHAPTER 2

Natalie took her strawberry daiquiri from the man, thanked him, and sipped it. "Nice." She turned to Virginia. "How's your piña colada?"

Virginia nodded. "Good. Now we know they have a good bar here." She turned to the men who were trying not to stare at her and Natalie. "Are you gentlemen here for the quilt retreat?"

The youngest of the three men, the tall athletic-looking man, shook his head. "No. We are here to do research."

Natalie drank more of her daiquiri then titled her head and asked, "Research? Are you academics or do you work for a company? What kind of research?"

The man stiffened. "We are… doing some independent studies. Archaeology."

"Archaeology? Something about the Seneca Indians?" Natalie asked.

"No. It has to do with some old developments on the lake."

"Sunken treasure from the pirate days?" Virginia asked. "Pirates were pretty active around this area in the 1700s."

"No, our research is based on an event in the 1920s."

Virginia looked at her drink, then said, "You're treasure hunters, aren't you? Looking for the lost 1923 gold coins?"

The tall athletic-looking man swallowed. "You know about the supposed treasure?"

"Sure. It's in our guidebook, and it's also popular local lore." Virginia finished her drink. "Good luck finding it."

"We'll need it." The man smiled. "I'm Jake Thompson." He swept his hand toward one of the other men. "This is Frank Jarvis." He noticed one of his friends eyeing Natalie. "And the fellow who can't seem to keep his eyes off this beautiful lady is Jason Ragget."

Virginia finished her drink. "I'm Virginia Davies Clark and my friend is Natalie North. We're quilters."

Jake smiled. "Nice to meet you, ladies. I take it you're not interested in the treasure."

Virginia shook her head. "It's been lost for a hundred years. Unless you have some new clues, why bother?"

Jason spoke up. "My great grandfather was one of the men that took the gold coins from the lake schooner *Midnight* in 1923. I'd like to locate the treasure."

Natalie moved next to him, *accidentally* brushed her breast against his arm and asked, "Did your great grandfather leave a journal or some written notes as to where it was supposed to go?"

"Yes. But he and the other men were murdered, and the coins were stolen before they could do anything with it."

"So, you have no clue as to where to start."

Frank cleared his throat. "Like Jason said, we have his great grandfather's notes, and in the notes, he mentions a name of someone who was also interested in obtaining the gold coins back then."

Virginia set her empty drink glass on a side table. "Have you found this person's relatives or know if he lived around here back in the 1920s?"

"Yes," Jake Thompson said.

"Good for you." Virginia gave Natalie a slight nod. "It's been nice meeting you gentlemen, and thank you, Jake, for the drinks. I'm sure we'll talk again soon. Now I think we should meet the other quilters."

She turned, and with Natalie next to her, started for the gathering of eight women across the room. "He's lying. He thinks his clue is suspect. He reminds me of a used car salesman in Encino, California on TV when I was in high school."

"I thought so, too." Natalie adjusted her tight red blouse and smiled as they approached the circle of women.

A woman in the circle, who appeared to be about seventy, cracked a smile and said, "Good afternoon, ladies. You must be Virginia and Natalie. I'm Ellen Croft. I'm the leader of the retreat this week. Welcome."

Virginia nodded. "Thank you. We're excited to be here." She glanced at the men then asked, "How did they manage to be staying here at the same time as the retreat?"

Ellen took a breath and sighed. "A computer glitch."

Natalie chuckled. "Fire your computer."

"I'm planning on doing just that. The operating system company helped me again and their update just... don't get me started."

One of the other women stepped closer. "We noticed you were talking to *those* men. Did they tell you about their treasure hunt?"

Virginia nodded.

She eyed Virginia's and Natalie's figures then said acidly, "I assume they asked *you two* to join them in their futile search."

Natalie lowered her voice and said in a nonspiritual tone, "No. They told us what they were going to do but didn't invite us to do anything. They did get us some drinks though. And if we were to go hunting for a missing treasure, we sure as hell wouldn't do it with them."

"I'm sure they'll ask you two to join them," said another woman caustically.

Virginia's patience had run out. "Look. We don't need your sarcasm. We just arrived. The men were nice to us, and as Natalie said, got us some drinks. If any of you have a problem with that, or us, speak up now so we can make other plans. For that matter, we could go treasure hunting on our own."

Ellen straightened to her full five-foot-two height and stated. "Ladies, Virginia and Natalie have come for the quilt retreat. I've seen examples of their work, and trust me, we could learn a few tricks from them. It is obvious why the men were… are attracted to them, but as Virginia said, they are here for the quilt retreat. They have been perfect ladies. Now stop acting catty and welcome them."

The other women swallowed and smiled, after which each greeted Virginia and Natalie.

A young lady stepped into the room and declared dinner was ready in the dining room.

Everyone filed into the room, decorated like a New England hunting lodge, and took seats around a long solid oak table. A fire burned in the hearth on the side. The ladies sat together at the end of the table closest to the large window overlooking the lake. The men sat a few chairs down the table.

Virginia looked around. The tension caused by the men being there was thick enough to cut with a knife. They ate dinner in relative silence until someone pointed at the window and announced it was raining. The discussion turned to the weather, old stories about pirates on Lake Ontario back in time, and fishing.

After dessert, a staff member entered, went to Ellen Croft, and whispered in her ear. Ellen's face drained of color. She stood. "Ladies and gentlemen, we have a sad development. One of the staff has just informed me that a body has been discovered in the woods above the old lighthouse."

Virginia stiffened. "Have the police been notified?"

"Yes. And they're here."

"Here? Why?"

"The police have identified the man as the local historian and amateur archaeologist, James St. Claire."

"Local? Does he live close by?" asked Natalie.

Ellen nodded. A small tear ran down her face. "He was such a nice man. A retired history teacher. He was researching something for the local Seneca Indians. It had to do with that old gold coin robbery in the twenties."

Natalie frowned. "Do the Indians own any land nearby?"

"Yes. A part of their local reservation juts up against my property behind the lighthouse."

"Isn't that where the gold coins were stolen for the second time, and the men were murdered in 1923?"

Ellen thought about it. "Close."

Virginia leaned back in her chair. "You said the cops are here? Where the body is or here at the retreat house?"

"Both. They want to talk to all of us. We need to adjourn to the parlor."

Natalie leaned toward Virginia. "Time to call The Smithsonian Central Security Service?"

Virginia sighed. "Yeah. Better tell our other employer in Washington, D.C. what's going on. Then I'll call my day-to-day employer, Dr. Doverspike, at the Georgetown Museum, so he doesn't get upset when he hears about it."

As the others rose, Virginia pulled her cellphone out and called the Smithsonian Central Security Service.

Her boss there, Special Agent Tom Mason, answered on the second ring. "Good evening, Virginia, to what do I owe the pleasure? You haven't killed anyone on your vacation yet have you?"

"No. I haven't killed anyone, yet. But—"

"Oh, no."

"Don't 'oh, no' just yet. I just wanted to tell you that I'm at a quilt retreat on the shore of Lake Ontario in New York."

"I know. What happened?"

"A body was found a short time ago near here on the Seneca reservation. It's a local historian and amateur archaeologist. James St. Claire." Virginia waited for a response, but Tom didn't say anything for a short time.

"It just came across my computer. The local Sheriff has notified the FBI, because the body was found on the Seneca reservation. This means a local pissing contest between the agencies."

"Tom, it has something to do with an old robbery of gold coins off a lake schooner in 1923."

"Hang on a second."

She heard him typing on his computer keyboard. Slowly, Tom spoke like he was reading something and talking. "Okay. Got it. You probably know as much about that robbery as I do. But since it has to do with the stolen U.S. gold coins, which are old and considered rare, as well as other possible antiquities *and* the Seneca Indians, I'm now putting you and Natalie on active duty; I take it she's there with you. You're now active-duty Special Agents and not reserve."

"We didn't bring our credentials or weapons. We're on vacation at a quilt retreat."

"I'm arranging for a courier to bring you everything you'll need. You'll have them in about an hour. But for now, go act like nice young quilters. Oh, and besides pissing off the other law enforcement folks and finding the killer, see if you can locate that gold and keep the body count down."

Virginia laughed. "Okay. Anything else you'd like? World peace?"

"That would be nice, but it'll never happen. I'll call Dr. Doverspike at the San Gabriel Museum and give him a substantial grant to cover for your time."

"He'll like that, especially since I'm on vacation. It isn't him I'm worried about."

"I'll smooth it over with your husband, Dr. Clark, and Natalie's guy, Dr. Jeff Cummings."

"Thanks, Tom. How long did you say before our badges, credentials, and weapons get here?"

"I notified the field office in Rochester to get them to you ASAP. Hang on a second..." Virginia could hear him talking on another phone then he returned. "Virginia, a federal marshal is on his way to you with everything you'll need. He should be there in a half hour."

"Let's hope the local sheriff and the FBI are still at each other's throats then and don't destroy the murder site. I'll call you after we have everything and take a look at the murder scene."

"Okay. Good hunting."

"We'll need it." She disconnected and glanced up as Natalie returned to the dining room.

Virginia swallowed. "What's wrong?"

CHAPTER 3

With a pensive expression, Natalie hurried across the room. She stopped in front of Virginia, took a deep breath then plopped in the chair next to her. She wet her lips, then said, "Those Keystone cops want to talk to us."

"Keystone cops?" Virginia frowned. "Why? We just got here."

"Someone told them we just arrived and went for a walk. Now this... this guy is found dead and the local sheriff and the... feather headed feds... FBI... are suspicious of us." Natalie calmed down. "How'd it go with The Smithsonian?"

"You and I are on active duty as of a few minutes ago. Someone is bringing us credentials, badges, and guns within the hour."

"That was fast."

"Yeah. The Smithsonian Central Security Service has a field office in Rochester, just to the west of us."

Virginia and Natalie turned as a short, round, uniformed sheriff's deputy and another man in a dark suit and curly black hair entered. Virginia whispered, "We'll be uncooperatively cooperative until our stuff arrives. Then we'll drop a bombshell on them."

Natalie grinned. "This'll be fun."

The deputy sheriff strutted up to Virginia and Natalie. "I'm Deputy Ferguson of the sheriff's office, and this is FBI Special Agent Jordan. We have a few questions for you."

Virginia sat back and crossed her arms. "Okay." She waited a few seconds then shook her head. "If you want to just stand there and stare at my friend's boobs, fine. But ask your questions first so you don't waste our time."

Agent Jordan's cheeks turned red. He cleared his throat. "I... we... understand that you two ladies arrived here a few hours ago. Is that true?"

Virginia nodded. "Yep."

"You're here for some sort of retreat?"

"Yep."

"You two went for a walk after you arrived. Is that correct?"

"Yep."

Jordan's eyes narrowed, his breathing became short and fast. "Can't you say anything but yep?"

Virginia chuckled. "Yep."

Agent Jordan shook his head and looked up from his notes. "Where did you go?"

"Why?"

Deputy Ferguson tensed, stepped closer, closed his notebook, and through clinched teeth said, "Listen, ladies. A man has been murdered. Now either answer the questions properly or we'll take you to the station for further interrogation. Got it?"

Virginia uncrossed her arms and leaned forward. "In that case we are done talking. You either let us go or arrest us. Got it?" She looked out the window, then back at the deputy. "Lawyer."

Deputy Ferguson and Agent Jordan exchanged bewildered expressions. Jordan motioned toward Ferguson to stand down then held up his hand. "No need for a lawyer. No one is going to arrest you. We are just trying to determine the whereabouts of everyone at the Inn." He gazed at Natalie again then grinned. "By any chance are you the actress, Natalie North?"

Natalie gave him a demure smile and nodded. "Yes. But I'm retired now and own a ranch in Texas."

Jordan's eyes widened. "Wow. That must be quite a change from Hollywood. I'm a big fan."

"You have no idea, and thank you for being a fan."

Everyone turned toward the door as a man in a bright green Polo shirt, tan slacks and with a gun and a round, silver badge on his belt entered carrying two metal cases. He walked up to the group. "I'm Deputy United States Marshal Seaborn. I have orders to deliver these cases to Special Agents Clark and North."

Virginia and Natalie stood. Virginia gave him a slight wave. "That would be us."

"Yes, ma'am. I need to see some ID, please."

Virginia and Natalie pulled their driver's licenses out of their pockets and handed them to the marshal.

Marshal Seaborn examined the licenses and then handed them back along with the cases. "Thank you, ladies." He glanced at the stunned FBI agent and deputy sheriff, then back at the women. "Have a nice evening." He turned and walked out.

The FBI agent and deputy sheriff watched as Virginia and Natalie stepped to the table, opened the cases, and took out their badge cases with their credentials and their weapons.

Virginia looked at the still quiet FBI agent. "Okay. We are special agents with the Smithsonian Central Security Service, and *we're* going to investigate the murder of James St. Claire."

Agent Jordan stammered at first, then said, "The body was found on an Indian reservation. That's a federal matter and under the purview of the FBI, not some museum guards."

Natalie moved close to him, took a breath, glared at him, then stated, "There are antiquities involved, the body is a federal matter, and in case you are hard of hearing, we are federal special agents, not museum guards. If you and your County Mounty friend have a problem with this, go call your bosses. We can work together, or you can just stay out of our way. That might be best. The last guys that got in our way… well at least one got to go to the hospital."

Deputy Ferguson swallowed. "What happened to the rest?"

Virginia shrugged. "Some went to the coroner. The others, well… their bodies never turned up."

Natalie smiled. "We've made men bigger than the two of you cry. So, if I were you, I'd treat us real nice. Cops or not, we do not like interference. But you play nice, and we'll play nice."

Agent Jordan put his notebook away. "I need to call this in."

Virginia nodded. "Okay. You boys go make your calls, finish questioning the other guests, and leave us alone while we get organized. We can compare notes in the morning."

Jordan gave a slight nod. "Okay. How about we come here about nine tomorrow?"

Virginia looked at Natalie, then said, "About nine? Okay. We'll have coffee and donuts available." She and Natalie sauntered out of the room.

"You're going to just let them walk out of here?" demanded Deputy Ferguson.

"Yes. They aren't going to be leaving any time soon, and I don't think we should piss them off. Working with them may be the best course of action. I'll make some calls and brief you as soon as I get confirmation about who they really are and their official status." Jordan glanced at the doorway. "And I think they were telling the truth about those people who got in their way."

"I don't know if I agree with this. I need to call my sergeant. I think we should hold them."

Jordan pointed. "Deputy, look out that window. What do you see?"

"Lake Ontario."

"Yeah. And it's big and deep. If *you* want to press the issue with those two women, go ahead. But *you* take the chance that they'll enjoy seeing how buoyant you are wearing concrete swim fins."

"I'm a police officer. They wouldn't do anything to me."

Jordan chuckled. "Your funeral."

"You believe them?"

"Hang on a moment." Jordan sat, pulled out his cellphone, and called his office. After a fifteen-minute conversation, he disconnected, put the phone away, and stared at the floor. He then glanced at the pacing deputy. "Washington says they are real federal agents and now have jurisdiction in this case. My boss also said to cooperate with them. He's already short of agents and doesn't need to lose another one. They may look like two harmless, beautiful blondes, but it seems these ladies have a habit of successfully completing cases that outstrips most agencies, even if they are a *little* unorthodox. They've been known to put very large and treacherous men into fetal positions, crying, and then go and get their nails done. My special-agent-in-charge said we're to work *with* them. In other words, play nice."

Deputy Ferguson looked at the doorway, took a breath, then asked, "You're saying those two... they're for real? They're federal agents? Wasn't that North woman an actress? How is she qualified to be here?"

"To quote Mrs. Clark, yep. And, for the record, I'm not questioning Ms. North's qualifications for anything. She went from being an actress, to owning a ranch in Texas, to a federal agent. Obviously, she's very capable."

"I guess you're right." Ferguson glanced around the empty room. "So, what do we do now?"

Jordan shrugged. "Looks like we finish interviewing all the others here at the Inn and then meet with Agent Clark and Agent North for coffee and donuts at nine tomorrow morning."

Deputy Ferguson rubbed his hands together. "I wonder what kind of donuts they'll have."

"It's what else they'll have that concerns me."

CHAPTER 4

Sunlight glistened off the smooth surface of Lake Ontario as Virginia slung her black backpack over her right shoulder. She munched on crispy Chinese noodles and followed Natalie up a dirt path to the place where the body was found. Virginia, in her blue Polo shirt and jeans, looked at her *Mickey Mouse* watch. It read seven thirty PM. "Lucky it's summer and still light." She glanced at the deputy sheriff guarding the crime scene. "We'd better introduce ourselves to that deputy before he gets all officious."

"Good idea." Natalie followed Virginia as they approached the deputy. "This'll be fun," she muttered.

Virginia, still holding the can of noodles, stopped in front of the officer and displayed her badge and credentials. "I am the lead officer on this case. We are going to inspect the body and the crime scene."

He looked at Virginia's badge then at her and Natalie in a tight green t-shirt and tan hiking shorts, her badge attached to her belt in front of her holstered gun. "I got a call on my radio about you two ladies a few minutes ago. My orders are to not get in your way."

"Good."

His eyes widened as he gazed at Natalie. "If you need anything, feel free to ask."

Natalie smiled. "We will. Thank you." She pointed to a stack of evidence bags in the deputy's crime scene case. "I could use a couple of those."

The deputy handed her several bags, and she turned to follow Virginia.

Virginia stepped toward the yellow police tape, placed the can with the noodles in her backpack, pulled out plastic gloves, and slipped them on. She knelt next to the body of amateur archaeologist, James St. Claire, nestled in dead maple, oak, and birch leaves and small broken tree branches. Virginia inhaled as the aroma of damp earth, oak leaves, and pine wafted into her nose. Virginia smiled then nodded toward the guard. "Natalie, keep an eye on that deputy over there standing guard."

"Okay." Natalie looked over Virginia's shoulder. "See anything of interest?"

"He has a knife wound in his chest just below his heart." Virginia opened his weathered tan messenger bag and removed what appeared to be a field notebook with a large rubber band securing it closed. "Put this in one of the evidence bags that deputy over there gave you."

"Okay." Natalie slipped the book into the bag, sealed it, and made the appropriate entries on the outside. "Find anything else?"

Virginia searched James St. Claire's pockets. "Wallet, driver's license, about twenty dollars in cash, and a picture of a woman." Virginia turned the picture over. "This must be Ann. No last name. There's a key ring with assorted keys, two pens and an arrowhead." She handed them to Natalie. "Do you have enough evidence bags for all that?"

"Yeah."

Virginia searched the messenger bag. "This is interesting." She removed two photographs and stood. "This picture is of the old lighthouse. This one is a photo of a quilt."

Natalie finished writing on the evidence bags then looked at the pictures. "That quilt has blue lighthouses and stars on it. There are also some notes scribbled on the picture. Think it's significant?"

Virginia stood. "It was tucked into a side pouch and zipped closed. So obviously he wanted to keep them safe. I need to study the picture of the quilt later."

"I'll turn these evidence bags over to that FBI agent when we see him in the morning. I suspect you're going to keep that picture of the quilt for us to use for the time being."

"I think we should also read what's in that field manual before we give it to the FBI and sheriff."

Natalie glanced around at the shafts of light filtering down through the myriad of leaves on the trees. "This area is surrounded by crime scene tape, and from what that deputy standing guard said, the forensic team and the coroner haven't been here yet. But someone has been searching the ground for something. Look at how the leaves and dirt are disturbed. That isn't from people just walking around. There is no way to identify the footprints."

Virginia looked where Natalie pointed. "Good call. You're right. Why would someone be searching this area unless it was our dead amateur archaeologist?"

"What would he be looking for?" Natalie looked at a squirrel watching them in the tree next to her. "You know, it could have been the killer searching for something our amateur archaeologist hid."

"I just thought of something."

Natalie tilted her head. "I know I shouldn't ask, but what?"

"That FBI agent and the deputy sheriff never told us who found the body."

Natalie frowned, then nodded. "You're right. They're holding out on us. We need to clear that up tomorrow morning when we meet them over coffee and donuts. But someone disturbed this area. The killer or our amateur archaeologist. Maybe the person who found the body did a little search on their own."

"Possibly. Right now, all the assumptions are valid. Maybe there's something in the notebook that'll give us a clue." Virginia continued to examine the area around the body then squinted. She moved closer to the base of a large maple tree, knelt, pushed some leaves aside, then picked up what appeared to be an old Iroquois or Seneca tomahawk. Attached to it was a tag with a number on it and the initials JSC. "Now this is significant. Our dead archaeologist must have hidden this before he was stabbed. Maybe that's why the area was disturbed. Someone was looking for it but was interrupted."

"Are we done here?" Natalie asked in a nervous voice.

"Yes. Why?"

"Good. The forensic people are coming up the hill and the coroner is behind them. What are we going to do with all this stuff?"

"Put it in our backpacks and casually walk down there and greet them."

"Okay."

Virginia and Natalie stepped across a brook on large, damp stones where they met the new group. After polite but strained greetings from the leader of the forensic team, Virginia and Natalie continued to the Inn.

Virginia sat at the round wooden table in their room at the Inn. She held a magnifying glass and examined the tomahawk. She glanced at Natalie, who was sitting on the sofa and reading James St. Claire's field notebook. "This tomahawk is Seneca. It dates from the late 1700s to the early 1800s. Why would this be important?"

"Does the blue stripe on the handle mean anything?"

"It was owned by a chief, or member of his family."

"Maybe that's all it is. Just an old artifact."

"Then why did he hide it, and why was someone looking for it?" Virginia took a photograph of it with her cellphone. "Anything in the notebook of interest?"

Natalie nodded. "I think so. James St. Claire mentions talking to a Seneca man, someone named John. They talked about an Indian woman who witnessed the gold robbers being shot back in 1929, the man who shot them, and his leaving with the truck containing the treasure."

Virginia dropped the tomahawk. "A woman was an eyewitness to the murders? Why didn't she come forward during the initial investigation back then?"

"It says here, John told James St. Claire that the woman, an elder tribesman's daughter, didn't trust the white man's police. She wasn't about to get involved. The local cops didn't treat the Indians very nice back then. Maybe that tomahawk belonged to her."

"That's very possible. Anything else?" Virginia asked.

"Yeah. She made a quilt that holds the secrets of the gold coins."

Virginia rose, stepped to the couch, and sat next to Natalie. "Does the journal say where the quilt is? What it looks like?"

"According to this, John, the Seneca man, gave James a picture of it. The quilt has lighthouses on it. And it's blue."

Virginia sprung to her feet and hurried to the table. She picked up the color photo of the lighthouse quilt. "This could be the picture. It's a digital color picture of a blue quilt with lighthouses, so it still exists. We need to locate this quilt."

Natalie set the book down. "It was made a hundred years ago. How are you going to find it now?"

"It's most likely still around here. Someone owns it but doesn't know its significance. This is a picture of it from this time. Maybe some of the quilters here at the retreat or in the area have seen it or own it. There are quilt stores around where quilters gather, share information, and gossip."

"It could still be on the reservation," Natalie added. "The woman's family may have it."

"True. But we have a real clue to follow up on." Virginia set the picture on the table. "Anything else in the book?"

"The name of the lead thief back in the 1920s. Ragget."

Virginia grinned. "The great grandfather of Jason Ragget, one of the men here looking for the gold. So he was telling the truth. But this notebook won't give him any information about who killed him and his men, or where the gold coins went."

"And he probably doesn't know about the Seneca woman who witnessed the murder or the quilt."

"Let's keep it that way for now," Virginia said.

"I have a question. Why didn't the killer go through James' messenger bag after he or she killed him? Why search for the tomahawk then leave?"

"Maybe someone was coming, and the killer fled before he had a chance. Someone found the body."

"Yeah, but who?" Natalie asked.

"Good question. We'll ask the FBI agent tomorrow morning."

"Are you going to turn all this over to the FBI and sheriff tomorrow like a good girl?"

"We'll give them the contents of James St. Claire's pockets, and the tomahawk."

"We're keeping the field manual and the quilt picture?"

Virginia glanced out the window at the lake then said, "Yes. We'll make up a field log, enter the descriptions of what we're keeping, give them the numbers for traceability, and then lock them up. We'd better put them back in their evidence bags, too, and reseal them. Nice and legal like."

"The FBI won't like that."

Virginia shrugged. "What they don't know won't hurt them, for now. Anyway, this treasure hunt and murder of a local amateur archaeologist makes me hesitant to trust the local authorities. And you and I are the lead investigators on this. Let's see how cooperative the FBI and sheriff really are."

"Then how do we find the quilt?" Natalie asked.

"Ask the locals about it. But don't tell them why we really want it."

"Right. We need to keep an eye on the treasure hunters that bought us drinks as well."

Virginia laughed. "That shouldn't be too hard. They seem more than taken with you."

Natalie's eyes widened. "Me! Oh, no you don't. I'm not playing footsy with that bunch."

"It's for a good cause."

Natalie crossed her arms and glared at Virginia. "Not buying it."

"Just be your normal, charming, sexy self. You'll have them eating out of your hands." Virginia snickered. "You may uncover some valuable intelligence for us."

Natalie pouted. "It's the uncover part I'm concerned about. They'll be thinking about me naked or under the covers."

"Think of this as another part in a Hollywood movie you're in, only this time with a little more wardrobe."

"Little more wardrobe?"

"Something conservative but revealing… sexy."

"That's… oh, hell. Conservative but revealing? Sexy? I'll see what I can come up with."

They jumped at the knock on the hall door.

CHAPTER 5

Virginia and Natalie exchanged glances. Virginia motioned to Natalie to put the evidence out of sight before she opened the door.

Natalie nodded, grabbed the evidence, and hurried to her bedroom.

Virginia opened the door and stared at a deputy sheriff standing in front of her. "Hello, deputy. What can I do for you?"

He straightened his posture, cleared his throat, and said, "The forensic team leader would like to talk to you, Agent Clark, and Agent North."

"Fine. When?"

"Now. He sent me to get you both."

Virginia eyed him. *The sheriff's people are trying to intimidate us. A power play. They don't like to be usurped in their territory. We need to address this now.* "Now is not convenient. You can tell the forensic team leader that we'll be meeting with Deputy Ferguson and FBI Special Agent Jordan in the morning. He needs to ask them if he can join us for coffee and donuts. We could meet with him later if he can't make the meeting."

"But… he…" The deputy stammered as Natalie stepped next to Virginia. Her blouse was loose and rolled up, exposing most of her bare breasts. This time she wore bright red shorts.

Natalie smiled at him. "Hi, deputy. I'm Natalie. What brings you here?"

"Ahh… I… I was just relaying a message." He swallowed. "Are you Agent North?"

"Yes," Natalie purred.

"Will you be at the meeting tomorrow with deputy Ferguson and Special Agent Jordan?"

Natalie leaned against the door frame and gave him an endearing look. "Yes. How about you, deputy? What's your name anyway?"

"Deputy Scott, ma'am. I… I think I'll be here or at the crime scene in the morning."

"Maybe I'll see you tomorrow." She glanced at Virginia who was trying to stifle a laugh. "If we're finished with deputy Scott, we still have some work to do."

Virginia nodded. "Deputy, please pass on my message to the forensic leader and hopefully we'll meet you again soon."

He pulled his eyes away from Natalie and nodded. "Yes, ma'am. I'll tell him." The deputy slowly walked down the hall toward the stairwell glancing over his shoulder at Natalie, who slowly reentered the room.

Virginia closed the door and stood with her hands on her hips. "That was a dirty trick to play on that young man. He'll need a cold shower."

Natalie laughed. "It was fun. Do you think this outfit would keep our treasure hunting guys occupied?"

"Oh, yeah. But with them maybe a little less exposure would be better. No telling where they might want to take you dressed like that." Virginia strolled back into the room. "You hid our evidence?"

"Yep. I was thinking, maybe we could start our discrete inquiries about the quilt tonight. According to the schedule, there is a social gathering of the ladies here going on downstairs now."

"Good idea. I would suggest you change, though. I don't think your attire would help getting information out of a bunch of women."

Natalie turned toward her bedroom. "I'll be right back."

Fifteen minutes later, Virginia and Natalie entered the parlor of the retreat house.

Ellen Croft, the leader of the quilt retreat, stepped up to them and handed them glasses of wine. "I understand you two are also federal agents and will be investigating the murder."

Virginia sipped some wine. "Yes. We're officially the lead investigators. But we'll also be taking part in the retreat."

"I hope so. If there's anything any of us can do to assist you with finding James St. Claire's murderer, we'll do it. He was a fine man and was loved by everyone around here."

Natalie eyed the hall leading toward the front door. "Are all the officials gone?"

Ellen glanced at the hallway. "You mean the police and forensic people?"

"Yes." Natalie drank some of her wine.

"They all departed a few minutes ago. One of them was not happy."

"He'll get over it. The sheriff and FBI aren't too happy either that Virginia and I took over the lead positions in the case."

"I understand." Ellen chuckled. "This is an election year for the sheriff, and I would think he's fit to be tied."

Virginia set her wine glass on a coaster on an end table. "Ellen, I have a picture I'd like to show you and the other ladies. But you must keep the fact that it exists under wraps. No one else is to know about it. Are you okay with this?"

"Will it help find James' killer?"

"We think so."

"We'll do whatever you want." Ellen turned. "Ladies, please come over here, Virginia and Natalie have something they need help with, regarding the search for James' killer."

The women scurried to join them. One of them, named Sue—according to her name tag—said, "What do you need?"

Ellen spoke quickly. "Virginia and Natalie have something to show us, and I promised them we'd keep it a secret, even from the sheriff, until they say it's okay. Agreed?"

They all agreed.

Virginia took the photograph of the blue lighthouse quilt from her pocket and displayed it to the women. "Do any of you recognize this quilt? Do you know where it might be now? Any history?"

The group of women stepped closer and examined the picture. One woman, who appeared to be in her late fifties, Lucille, nodded. "I know that quilt."

Another lady, in her early thirties, Nancy, added, "Me too. That's the old Seneca woman's quilt."

Natalie almost choked on her wine. "That was fast. Almost too fast. Do you know where it is now?"

Nancy and Lucille shook their heads. Lucille sighed. "Last I saw it was at our quilt show last year. A young woman entered it in the show. It was for display and wasn't judged."

Virginia smiled. "Do you know this woman's name?"

"No. She isn't a member of our guild. But we can look up her name. It's in the quilt guild's show records."

"And who has these records?"

"I do," said Ellen. "They're in the basement where my quilt room is. If it's important, then let's go down there and take a look."

The group followed Ellen through the first floor and to the cellar stairs. After switching on the lights, they climbed down to the finished basement. A few steps down a wide hall was a door with a small, quilted wall-hanging of a star. The door was ajar. The light was on inside.

Ellen stopped. "That door was locked, and I know I turned off the lights."

"Stay here." Virginia and Natalie pulled semiautomatic handguns from seemingly nowhere and cautiously inched forward. Virginia silently pushed the door open with her foot and peered around the corner. The room, cluttered with fabric pieces, quilting tools, cutting boards, a design wall, and a large sewing machine, stood apparently empty. Just as she was about to enter, she heard a sound from the closet at the rear of the room.

Virginia edged cautiously into the room, skirted the ironing board and sewing machine table, then approached the closet. The sounds from the closet were that of boxes falling, paper being torn, and something or someone moving. Virginia motioned for Natalie to stand behind the sewing machine just off to the right of the door. When Natalie was in place, Virginia pushed the handle down and yanked the door open. A cat jumped back, snarled, then bolted from the closet.

"Bob! How'd you get in that closet?" yelled Ellen Croft. She scooped up the gray cat as it stormed out of the quilt room.

Natalie moved to the hall door and raised an eyebrow. "Bob?"

Ellen chuckled. "Bob Cat is his name."

"Cute. How'd he get in there? Was he already in the closet when you left?"

"I don't think so. Anyway, I closed and locked the quilt room when I left it last night, and I know I turned off the lights."

Virginia knelt in front of the door and examined the lock. "The lock was picked." She stood. "Someone entered that room and looked around. The closet is a mess. Ellen, please look and see if anything is missing. The cat wasn't happy in there, and he tore some things up."

The women gathered around the door and glanced inside, then at Virginia's and Natalie's pistols. One of the ladies asked where they had hidden them. Virginia chuckled. "Under our blouses."

Ellen walked through the quilt room and into the walk-in closet. After a couple minutes, she called out from the closet. "Bob didn't do all this. Someone emptied out three notebooks. They didn't get much of interest except some old quilt and purse patterns. Someone was looking for something."

Natalie hurried to the closet. "Are the records for the quilt show among the things in those notebooks?"

Ellen shook her head then pointed at a small cabinet in the quilt room. "No. They're in that cabinet."

Virginia examined the cabinet. It had a simple door with no handle or latch. She opened it. Nothing seemed out of place. She turned toward the closet. "Ellen, can you see if anything was disturbed in here and if you can find the woman who owns the quilt Natalie and I are looking for?"

Ellen stepped around a stack of quilt magazines on the floor to get to the cabinet. She stooped and fished out a blue 8x10 binder. "I think this is the right one." She set it on the sewing table and thumbed through plastic sleeves with forms in them.

Natalie moved closer. "Find anything?"

"No. Not yet." Ellen kept going through the plastic pages until she was near the end. "Here it is." She opened the rings, pulled out the sleeve and handed it to Natalie. "This is it. I hope this helps. The show was last year. We have them every other year."

"Virginia," one of the women called. "There are two men coming down the stairs."

CHAPTER 6

Virginia heard the footfalls on the steps. "I'll handle this."

Natalie moved next to Virginia and placed her hand on her shoulder. "You assigned me to handle the guys, remember. I seem to have sparked something in them."

"Yeah, I know what you sparked. Okay, go torture their libidos."

Natalie adjusted her blouse, wound through the group of women, and marched to the bottom of the stairs just as the two men reached the basement. "Hello, fellas. What brings you down here?"

They stopped and stared at Natalie. Grins quickly appeared on their faces. One of the men, Jason Ragget, swallowed and then said, "Ahh... we heard a commotion down here and thought we'd take a look. You know, in case there was a problem." He tried to peer around her.

Natalie shifted to block his view. "There's nothing down here to interest you guys. No treasure or anything related to the gold coins. Just Ellen's quilt room. We came down to see it. Her cat got stuck in the closet and made a fuss."

The men tried to step around her, but Natalie moved to block them each time. Then she took a deep breath which stopped them in their tracks. She gave them a demure smile. "Why don't you gentlemen take little ole me up to the bar, and let's have some drinks."

They looked at each other, shrugged, and nodded. Jake Thompson said, "That works for me."

"Okay, then, lead the way fellas." Natalie waved at Virginia and followed the men up the stairs.

Ellen turned frantically to Virginia. "Will she be okay alone with those men? They seem a little suspicious to me and maybe dangerous."

"Not to worry. Natalie will have them under her spell by the time they get to the top of the stairs. If they do try anything she doesn't like, well, I pity them. She also has a 9mm under her blouse," stated Virginia. She looked around, "Who has the information from the notebook?"

Ellen's face drained of color. "Natalie."

"Oh, good lord. She took it with her. I'll let you ladies straighten up here, and I'll go help Natalie." She hurried for the stairs.

Virginia bounded up the steps and followed the sound of voices to the kitchen. She stopped at the doorway and stared. Natalie, with a tall drink in her hand, leaned against the wall in a pose that obviously inspired sexy thoughts in the minds of the three men sitting at the table. They were all trying to talk to her at once. Virginia bit her lip. *How did Natalie get that drink so fast? Should I be worried?* Virginia took a quick breath then entered the kitchen. The men turned toward her.

Jake Thompson smiled. "Well guys, we've got another beauty joining us. What'll you have to drink, Virginia?"

"Nothing right now, thank you. But I need to talk to Natalie for a minute."

Before anyone could say anything, Natalie pushed off the wall and walked toward Virginia. She glanced over her shoulder and said, "I'll be right back, fellas. Don't go anywhere." She followed Virginia into the hall. "What's up?"

"You have the picture of the quilt and the name and address of the owner on you. Being with the men over there could jeopardize things."

Natalie chuckled. "Come with me." She stepped to a narrow table in the hall with a large decorative urn on it. The urn sat on a quilted table runner. Natalie picked up the end and pulled out the plastic sleeve with the information in it and handed it to Virginia. "I slipped it under here when they led me to the kitchen. They never saw it."

Virginia sighed. "Good. I should have known you'd be devious."

"Yes, you should. Now I have to go cause them to have sweet dreams tonight."

"Sweet dreams? What are you going to do?"

"I was an actress remember? They'll be happy and dream of me in sexy, nasty ways, while in reality I didn't do a thing. I do have a boyfriend I love, so I'll fake it." Natalie glanced at the kitchen door when one of the men called her. "I'd better get back to work. Put that information in a safe place and come back. I'm sure they'd be more than happy to have you join us." She turned and sashayed to the kitchen.

Virginia looked at the plastic sleeve with the picture and information sheet in it, then shook her head. *I'd better hide this and join Natalie before she either causes a heart attack or they do something she's not ready for.* She stood for a moment looking at the kitchen doorway. *It isn't her I need to worry about. She may be shorter than Tom Cruise, but she is dangerous.*

CHAPTER 7

In her suite, Virginia slid the plastic sleeve with the lighthouse quilt information in it under her mattress. She turned and walked into the parlor area of the suite when she heard a noise at the door to the hallway. She drew her pistol, stepped to the door, and peered out through the peephole. Outside stood Frank Jarvis, one of the three treasure hunters. *What's he doing here? Where's Natalie?* Virginia held her gun behind her back and swung the door open. "Mr. Jarvis, what are you doing here? I thought you'd be with your friends."

"I was. But Jake Thompson and Jason Ragget have taken your cute friend Natalie outside and down toward the lake." He glanced around nervously. "Jason can't seem to get her out of his mind. I thought I'd better come and get you."

"Why? Do they intend to do something to her?"

He wet his lips. "I don't think so, but Jason is infatuated with her, especially since he looked her up on the Internet and found those provocative pictures from her movies. And he's slightly drunk. In his present state of mind..." He fidgeted with his hands. "I thought I'd better come get you."

Virginia frowned. "You left them with her to get me?"

"Ah, yes. We need to go see what they are up to."

"Wait here a moment while I shut down my computer."

Virginia closed the door, slid her gun back into its holster under her blouse. *Something is up. He's way too nervous for just worrying about Natalie. I figure now someone will look for my computer. These guys are amateurs. If they try something with Natalie... I hope their health insurance is paid up.* She adjusted her blouse and reopened the door. "Let's go. Lead the way."

She followed Frank down the hall and stairs, then out through the dining room doors into the moonlit night. As she walked, she could hear the washing of the small waves of the lake on the beach below and the sound of crickets.

"I think they're down by the old pier that was part of the lighthouse.

It's just ahead," stated Frank.

Virginia tilted her head, listening. *I don't hear anyone talking. This feels wrong.* She followed Frank down stone steps toward the lake. She could see the outline of the old lighthouse against the sky. Frank started to slow and stopped a few feet in front of her. He turned toward her, pulling a small silver revolver from under his shirt. Virginia quickly drew her gun, thumbed off the safety, and aimed at him. "Drop the gun, Frank. Get down on your knees with your hands on top of your head."

He stood for a moment then lowered his weapon. His eyes were cold as he stared at Virginia. "You're not going to shoot anyone."

"Why not?"

"Because you don't have the guts. It takes a lot to shoot someone." He raised his weapon. Virginia's pistol fired. Stunned, he staggered back when the bullet hit him in his side. He dropped to the ground.

Virginia stepped to him. "Put the gun down or the next shot will kill you."

Through clenched teeth, Frank muttered, "I can't believe you'd do that." Perspiration beaded on his forehead. He dropped the gun and held his side as blood oozed out between his fingers. "I need a doctor."

Virginia chuckled. "Yeah, you do. Why don't you call for the paramedics?"

His body wavered. "I can't. Please… call for help."

"Where did your friends take Natalie?"

"I need a doctor."

"You already said that." She glared at him. "Where is Natalie?"

"In the basement of the old lighthouse. That's where I was to take you."

Virginia put her gun away, pulled out her phone, and hit speed dial for Special Agent Mason at the Smithsonian Central Security Service. When he answered she said, "Before you ask, Tom, he isn't dead yet."

"Who isn't dead yet? You shot someone or just removed part of his anatomy?"

"The guy I just shot pulled a gun on me and was going to kidnap me."

"Not smart. Are you okay?"

"I'm fine but I need to go rescue Natalie. The guy I shot is at the retreat location, down a path toward the lake and the old lighthouse. He needs paramedics. He's bleeding."

"Okay. I'll get the clean-up medical team out to your location. Go do what you need to do for Natalie."

"I'll use plastic ties to bind him to a tree, just in case."

"I've got our paramedics and clean-up crew en route. They'll look like real paramedics and real sheriff's deputies."

"Okay." She hung up and looked at Frank. "Help is on the way. Now move close to that maple tree. I'm going to tie you to it."

He looked at Virginia through burning eyes. "I'm not moving."

Virginia shrugged. "Have it your way." She pulled out her gun and aimed it at his crotch. "This will hurt you more than me. Trust me, they'll hear you scream in Canada all the way across the lake."

"Okay, okay. I'll move." Moaning, he inched his way to the tree.

Virginia pulled a few plastic Zip-Cuffs and Zip Cable Ties from her pocket to secure him to the tree. When she was finished, she patted his head and said, "Now be a good boy and wait for the medics and the sheriff." Sounds of footfalls coming from the retreat building caused Virginia to stand and draw her weapon. She lowered it when Ellen Croft came down the steps alone.

Ellen stopped and looked at Frank. "Virginia, what happened? I thought I heard a gunshot. He's bleeding."

"You did. Frank here drew a gun on me. I was a little faster." She chuckled under her breath. "The sheriff and paramedics are coming."

Ellen shook her head. "What a stupid thing for him to do. Why?"

"The treasure."

"Oh. I see." Ellen looked at Frank again then at Virginia. "Where is Natalie?"

"With the others. I'm going to go get her."

"I can stay and watch him until the authorities arrive," Ellen said.

"Thank you." Virginia picked up Frank's gun and tucked it into her waistband. "I shouldn't be long." She hurried down the path toward the lake.

Ellen watched Virginia disappear down the path into the trees, then knelt next to Frank. "What were you thinking? I didn't authorize this. Now look what you've done. Those women are feds and now even more alert."

"I didn't think she'd do it."

"How much do Jason and Jake know?"

"Nothing. I didn't tell them anything," said Frank with a quivering voice. "You have to get me out of this."

"The medics will take you to the hospital and get you patched up. The sheriff will lock you up. You'll be safer in jail than tangling with Virginia and Natalie. Just don't talk to the sheriff or FBI. I'll get you out."

Frank swallowed. "Okay."

Ellen turned at the sound of sirens approaching. "Help is here. Remember, no talking, and I'll protect you. Open your mouth, and..." she pointed, "that's a big, cold, and deep lake... got it?"

CHAPTER 8

Virginia rushed down the gravel path toward the lake and the lighthouse. Nearing the base of the structure, she stepped into the trees and observed her surroundings from behind a large oak tree. *No sign of Natalie or the other two guys. This is obviously a trap.* A slight breeze caused the leaves to rustle overhead. She pulled out her phone and did an unsuccessful Google search for information about the lighthouse, especially any floor plans. She closed her phone and watched the only door on the lower section of the building. After a minute, Virginia spotted light under the door. She pulled her sidearm, crouched, and quietly hurried to the side of the door, flattening herself against the wall. She leaned to her side and put her ear close to the door listening for sound and jumped when a noise came from just inside. Virginia stepped back. *What the hell was that?* She reached for the door handle when it swung open. Virginia brought her gun up then stopped. She stared at Natalie. "Natalie? Are you okay?"

"I'm fine." Natalie glanced around. "What's with the sirens?"

"They're for a mock paramedic and sheriff's team that's coming for Frank Jarvis."

"Mock paramedics and… oh… they're from the Smithsonian… a clean-up team," Natalie said. "What did Frank do to warrant such help?"

"He pulled a gun on me."

"Yeah, that'll do it. I take it you shot him. Is he dead?"

"Yes, I shot him. And no, I only wounded him. But he will disappear." Virginia looked behind Natalie down a semi-lit corridor. A power line was strung from the ceiling with light bulbs at intervals. "What are you doing down here, and where are Jason Ragget and Jake Thompson?"

Natalie stepped back. "Come on in. I'll show you." She turned and led Virginia down a short corridor to a room with a single overhead light strung from the ceiling casting shadows about as it swayed.

Jason Ragget and Jake Thompson sat at an old, rickety wooden table under the light bulb.

Virginia strolled into the musty room and stood next to the table. "You two trying to worm information about our investigation out of Natalie?"

Jake laughed. "That was our plan, but Natalie was better at extracting information from us than we were at getting anything from her."

Jason held up an old, dog-eared notebook. "Natalie even got us to share what's in my grandfather's notebook. I'm sorry to say we underestimated this little lady."

Virginia smiled. "Most men underestimate her. So, this meeting was like an interrogation that went the other way."

The two men nodded.

Virginia pulled up a chair of questionable stability and sat. "How about the murder of the amateur archaeologist, James St. Claire?"

"We didn't have anything to do with that," Jake said. "We're not killers. We heard about it the same time you did. We didn't even know the man."

Virginia gave a slight nod. "I see."

Jake glanced at the door. "Where's Frank? He was supposed to go get you to join us."

"Oh? He won't be joining us. Your friend Frank Jarvis pulled a gun on me."

Jake's eyes widened. "He did what?"

"Pulled a gun on me."

Jake looked bewildered. "Why?"

Jason shook his head and spoke before Virginia could answer. "Probably because Frank always was a hothead. He's been acting strange lately. Secretive. He makes secret calls on his cellphone. When we ask about them, he changes the subject. He's gotten worse since we heard about that archaeologist fellow's death. Jake and I don't even have any guns. We didn't kill that archaeologist either. If he pulled a gun on you, and you're here and he isn't, then… did you shoot him? Is he dead?"

"Yes, I shot him, but no, he isn't dead. He's being treated by medics and will sort of disappear."

Jason frowned. "Sort of disappear?"

"You won't see him again. For everyone around here, he doesn't exist anymore." Virginia watched Natalie pull up a chair across from her. "So, did you learn anything from the journal?"

Natalie ran her fingers through her blonde hair and shook her head. "Just what we already knew. But there *is* a name in the notes of someone who was also interested in obtaining the gold coins back then."

"Who was he?"

"Graham Weedon," Jason stated.

Natalie leaned forward. "I asked if they knew anything about him or who and where any existing relatives might be."

Jason spoke. "We haven't had any luck finding anyone who knew him. We don't know where he lived or who he is."

Virginia smiled. "You're at a dead end. But maybe we can help with that lead."

"That would be great. Thank you." He knitted his brow. "Why are you helping us?"

"We'd like to recover the gold coins, too. However, we have a murder to solve, and it seems the two are related."

"In that case, can we help with the murder investigation?" Jason asked.

Virginia looked across the table at Natalie typing on her cellphone. "Are you sending a request for information about Graham Weedon to Washington?"

Natalie nodded then turned to the men. "I'll kill two birds with one stone, so to speak. Where are you two from?"

Jake wet his lips. "Why?"

"It may make the background check on you two I've requested run faster."

"I'm from Rochester. Jason's from Irondequoit. It's a suburb of Rochester. We both work at Kodak."

"I know where Irondequoit is," Natalie said as her fingers flew across the phone's little keyboard. She looked up at the men. "Does Frank live near you fellas?"

"Yes," Jake replied. "He lives in Rochester as well. He's a member of the country club I belong to. We've played golf together in foursomes. That's how we met."

Virginia sat back. "To set the record straight from the start, why exactly are you guys after the gold coins? The family connection, or is someone else behind your search?"

"We came after the coins on our own," Jason said. "The missing coins have been a legend in my family for decades. I have my grandfather's journal where he discusses it and had the name Graham Weedon in it. Jake and I took some time off to come here and see what we could find."

"How about Frank?" asked Virginia.

Jake cleared his throat, then said, "Frank hooked up with us just before we left to come here. He has some family in the area, and Jason and I figured having someone from around here might help. He said he had some money someone gave him to help find the coins. I guess we should have given his nervousness, the money donation, and his attitude more attention."

"Probably would have been a good idea." Virginia's face turned dark. "Someone gave him money to find the coins. Who?"

Jason shook his head. "Frank wouldn't tell us."

Natalie put her phone down. "The questions are, who killed the archaeologist and why, who's paid Frank to find the gold coins, and how are they related?"

Jason nodded, then said, "And why did Frank want to kidnap or shoot Virginia?"

Virginia flexed her fingers. "I have another question. Have either of you gentlemen heard about anyone around here named John?"

Jake shook his head. "I haven't. But we haven't been here very long."

Jason agreed, then asked, "What's John's last name?"

Virginia sighed. "We don't know."

Natalie chuckled. "We got this mysterious John, Graham Weedon, and no reason why Frank would want to harm Virginia, as well as a very dead archaeologist."

"And a missing quilt." Virginia put her fingers to her lips and rose. As she turned, Ellen Croft entered the room and stopped.

Ellen smiled. "There you all are. I'm glad I found you. We've got refreshments out up at the Inn."

Virginia turned back to the table. "Maybe we should join the others and enjoy the evening."

Jake, Jason, and Natalie quickly rose and headed for the door. Virginia stepped behind Natalie with Ellen at her side.

Ellen leaned close. "The paramedics came along with a state trooper and took Frank."

Virginia nodded. "Good."

"When I asked which hospital and what jail they were going to take him to, they didn't answer. I made some calls and none of the hospitals around here have Frank."

Virginia chuckled. "How about that."

"Virginia, what's going on?"

"A murder investigation, a treasure hunt, and some weird shenanigans by a person or persons unknown."

"But what happened to Frank?"

"He's part of the shenanigans. I'd hate to be the person behind all that. Trust me, Natalie and I are good at stopping crime, finding bad guys, and they usually go to jail."

"Usually?"

"The others either disappear forever or get killed." Virginia glanced at Ellen. "You wouldn't be involved, would you?"

Ellen swallowed. "Disappear or killed. That... that sounds ominous."

"I promise you, Natalie and I will get to the bottom of all this one way or another... and soon."

Ellen, with her head down, shuffled behind Virginia out of the old lighthouse.

CHAPTER 9

Virginia and Natalie nibbled on some fruit, cheese, and crackers, sipped some white wine, then excused themselves. They approached Ellen. "It's getting late, and we still have some work to do. We're going to adjourn to our suite."

Ellen smiled. "It has been an exciting first day. After this, I too want to retire early."

"Did you arrange for the donuts and coffee for tomorrow when we meet with the FBI and Sheriff? Will we have a variety of donuts like I requested?" Natalie asked.

"Yes. Everything will be ready in the parlor a little before nine."

"Excellent. Well, good night." Natalie followed Virginia out of the room.

In their suite, Virginia retrieved the plastic binder folder and pulled out the picture of the lighthouse quilt. On the back was printed the owner's name, address, and phone number. "The name on this is Victoria Longfellow. She lives on Queensboro Road in Irondequoit, New York," Virginia said.

"You said there's a phone number?"

"Yep."

"What is it? I'll give her a call now."

"It's late."

"It's only quarter to ten. If she isn't up or isn't there, I can leave a message."

"Okay. The number is 585-555-9378. Give it a try."

Natalie poked at her cellphone then waited. She sat up straight when a woman answered. "Hello?"

Natalie smiled at Virginia. "Is this Victoria Longfellow?"

"Ahh... yes. Who are you?"

"I'm Special Agent Natalie North with the Smithsonian Central Security Service. We have a picture of a quilt you entered in a quilt show last year."

"Are you police?"

"Federal agents. We'd like to meet you and see that blue lighthouse quilt, if you still have it. I know you don't know us, and probably haven't heard of our agency, but we're investigating a murder and some missing artifacts. We can meet anyplace you want, and any time except tomorrow morning from nine to twelve. Do you still have the quilt?"

"Yes, I have the quilt. Can I bring a friend?" Victoria asked in a hesitant voice.

"You can bring as many people as you like. Bring the sheriff if you want to."

"Okay. Where are you?"

"We are at a quilt retreat on the Lake Front Highway at an old, dilapidated lighthouse—"

"You're at Ellen Croft's retreat center?" Victoria asked.

"Yes," Natalie responded.

"Good. I can come there tomorrow. I'll bring John with me. He may know more about the quilt than I do. What time would be convenient?"

"Wonderful. Say, one-thirty?"

"One-thirty it is. See you then, Agent North."

Natalie disconnected and looked at Virginia who was pacing. "We're set up tomorrow—"

"Victoria Longfellow is coming here at one-thirty."

Natalie shook her head. "Eavesdropping again, I see. But what you didn't hear is she is bringing the mysterious John with her." Natalie stared at the ceiling, then at Virginia. "Isn't he the man from James St. Claire's notebook? I remember a mention of a Seneca man named John."

"Yes, and that's good news." Virginia picked up her cellphone. "I'll call Special Agent Mason and have him arrange a security detail for Victoria from now until she reaches us with that quilt."

"You think that's necessary?"

"Based on events up to now." Virginia's expression was one of uneasy puzzlement. "I don't want anything happening to that quilt or Victoria. This is just a precaution."

"Better safe than sorry."

Virginia pushed the speed dial for Tom's home number. He answered with a grumpy tone. "I figured it was you at this hour. My favorite agent again disturbing my sleep. What do you need? Shoot someone else tonight?"

Virginia smiled at his comment. "No, Tom, we haven't shot, maimed, or hurt anyone else tonight. But we have a big lead on the case."

"You could have told me that in the morning."

"Natalie and I want her alive and here tomorrow, and we want the lighthouse quilt she has."

"Okay, let me get my notebook… okay, what's the lady's name, and where does she live?"

Virginia provided Tom the information and what she hoped to find in the quilt. She listened and then hung up. "He'll have agents around her house within a half hour, and they'll shadow her here tomorrow as well."

Natalie nodded. "And if someone tries to interfere with the lady and the quilt?"

"They'll be picked up and held until you and I can question them."

Natalie's face lit up. "Oh… goodie!"

Virginia gave her a stern expression. "You can't waterboard him."

"Party pooper." Natalie sat back in the chair near the window. "Do we pass this new development on to the sheriff and FBI in the morning?"

"Let's see what they have first. I'm not impressed with the FBI, and I don't know if there's any relationship between anyone here and the sheriff's people."

"You suspect someone at the retreat… besides the two guys we talked to?" Natalie asked.

"Right now, I suspect everyone. Oh, I forgot to mention, Tom got the background report on the three treasure hunters."

"Okay. Are they criminals? Maybe international antiquity thieves?"

"Jake Thompson and Jason Ragget are clean. No arrests, not wanted for anything, and no outstanding warrants. They're reported to be honest family men. Jason is a boy scout leader. The two treasure hunters are probably exactly as they appear."

Natalie frowned. "And your friend Frank Jarvis?"

"He has a record. Nothing serious, a couple misdemeanors when he was a teenager. He was suspected of involvement in a smuggling ring transporting drugs across the border from Canada, but there was insufficient evidence to arrest him. He has a serious financial problem now—gambling. He likes it but isn't good at it. Owes some nasty people a lot of money. He works for a clothing manufacturer in Rochester. He's a member of a country club and loves golf."

"If he's in financial trouble, why is he still a member of the country club? They aren't cheap."

"You can ask him when you… interview him… without inflicting pain."

"You're no fun. Anyway, I have never actually tortured or hurt anyone. I just plant the idea of what I'm going to do to them in their mind, and they're more than happy to answer my questions." She cupped her ample breasts. "Sometimes I use the girls, and that gets me my answers."

Virginia chuckled. "You are good, I'll give you that."

Virginia's cellphone rang with the Pirates of the Caribbean theme song. She picked up her phone and looked at the caller ID. "This may not be good news." She answered it and listened. Her face fell as she plopped down on the chair.

CHAPTER 10

Virginia listened, nodded, and listened more. Then she asked, "So Victoria Longfellow's okay?"

"Yes. We took her and the man who was with her named... John... no last name so far, and the quilt into protective custody," said her boss, Tom. "She said he was with her and needed him when she sees you."

"Where do you have them?"

"Somewhere safe but close to you. Here's the cell number of the agent in charge. Tell him where you want her, John, and the quilt to be and when. He'll be expecting your call tomorrow."

Virginia copied down the phone number and the special code for identification. "Okay, thanks, Tom. What about the person who tried to break into her house?"

"Don't worry about him. And tell Natalie she won't need to interrogate him either."

"He's dead?"

"Yes. He tried to knife one of our agents."

"I'm glad we don't have to be concerned about him. He was probably just the hired help. Who was he? Did he say anything?"

"He was an up-and-coming gang member from Buffalo. You're right, cheap, stupid, and overconfident. Thug for hire. Besides swearing at our agents when he was shot, he didn't offer anything of value before he died."

"Okay, I'll tell Natalie. Thanks for the update."

"Be on your guard. Someone is playing hardball."

Virginia ended the call and looked at Natalie. "Some cheap thug tried to attack Victoria and take the quilt. Our special agents on site killed him."

Natalie sat wide-eyed. "Is Victoria okay?"

"Yes." Virginia relayed the story to Natalie, then sat back in her chair. "Tom said to watch our sixes—our backs."

Natalie slowly nodded. "Somehow there's a leak from here. Maybe we shouldn't use the house phones. We need to find the leak and plug it. And Tom has a good idea about protecting our rear flanks. We're going to talk to that FBI guy and the County Mounty tomorrow at nine. Let's lock up and get some rest but sleep with our guns."

At breakfast, seven the next morning, Virginia noticed an air of curiosity and caution in the dining room. The quilters were all chatty about the shooting and the missing man Frank Jarvis. They eyed the other two men there with suspicion. At first, they questioned Virginia and Natalie about what happened, but they figured out they weren't going to get much information and went back to eating and discussing aspects of quilting.

After they finished eating, Virginia and Natalie went to the parlor. They found Ellen putting the finishing touches on the tray with the donuts, the coffee urn, the mugs, sugar bowl, creamers, and dishes. She had arranged the chairs and sofa so they faced the brick fireplace.

Ellen gave Virginia a hopeful smile. "Is this okay?"

Virginia walked into the room and looked at the setup. "Perfect. We should be able to keep things civil with all these donuts and the coffee. Thank you, Ellen. This is above and beyond the call of duty."

"I want you two ladies to find out who killed James St. Claire and arrest him. If you can locate the old gold coins… well, that would be a plus. By the way, if you find the coins, who owns them?"

Virginia frowned. "I'm not sure. Maybe the owner of the land where they're found, or the original owner if still alive, or the state or federal government. I'm not a lawyer, so I don't know."

"Oh. I was curious."

"That's a lot of money, so I bet everyone is now interested," Virginia added.

Ellen chuckled. "Yes, so expect constant questions later." She hurried out of the room.

Natalie turned from the window. "Guess who's here? Our favorite fuzz or fuzzes. What's the plural of fuzz?"

"I don't know. Let them in. Everything is ready."

After brief pleasantries, they took assorted donuts and mugs of coffee to their chairs and set them on the wooden TV trays in front of the chairs.

Deputy Ferguson spoke first. "I understand there was a shooting here yesterday." He consulted his notes. "A Mr. Frank Jarvis was shot, but our office was not notified. It seems Mr. Jarvis has gone missing as well as being shot. Reports are that some mysterious medics and a nonexistent state trooper took him away. You two know anything about this?"

Natalie took a bite of her donut and shrugged her shoulder. "How'd you find out?"

"A concerned citizen reported it to us."

"You are correct." Virginia took a sip of coffee and set the cup down. "Mr. Jarvis pulled a gun on me. I shot him. He is now receiving medical treatment and is locked in a secure location pending interrogation."

Ferguson leaned forward. "This is a local police matter, and he has certain rights. This is something for the sheriff's office to investigate." He drank some coffee. "Please turn him over to us at the earliest. Where is he?"

"He is somewhere safe, so he won't bother us while we investigate the bigger crime. You'll get him when we're done with him."

Ferguson started to rise when FBI Special Agent Jordan put his hand on the deputy's arm. "Relax, deputy. Sit back down. They'll surrender Mr. Jarvis when they're done with him. We have orders to cooperate with these two nice ladies, don't piss them off."

Ferguson relaxed. "Yes. You're right. Just the deputy sheriff in me getting excited."

"No problem." Virginia finished her donut. "Okay boys, what have you got for us?"

Special Agent Jordan thumbed through his notes. "Last night, we ran background checks on the women here. Nothing stood out. A few have had some traffic tickets but that's about it."

Natalie stared at the donuts remaining on the tray then took another glazed one. "How about the men here?"

"They were clean except the fellow Virginia shot. He's a piece of work. But he isn't wanted for anything now. I also ran the background of the murder victim, amateur archaeologist James St. Claire." Ferguson shook his head slightly. "He seems to be a strange individual." Ferguson finished his donut then sipped some coffee.

"How so?" Virginia asked.

"For an amateur, he has quite a reputation as a good field archaeologist and relic hunter. He spends most of his time working on the Native American cultures in the upstate New York area and New England. He has uncovered countless relics and artifacts, and he takes careful notes and turns them over to the Seneca Indians or the proper authorities. Some of his finds are worth a lot of money, but he ensures they are cataloged and given to the tribes or museums. He has a civil engineering degree from the Rochester Institute of Technology and a master's degree in anthropology from The State University of New York at Buffalo. He also has a graduate diploma in archaeology from The University of Chicago. He was a full-fledged nerd."

Natalie tilted her head. "What does… did he do for a living?"

Special Agent Jordan responded, "He got grants and commissions for his archaeology, speakers fees for talking to groups, and owned a consulting engineering company."

"Anything that hints of corruption?"

"Nothing. He's got a clean record and was considered a nice guy, but a geek."

"Was he married?"

"He was married. Wife got tired of him and his relics, was bored, wanted more excitement and better sex, and found a new younger squeeze. She was a looker but not bright. Mr. St. Claire found out about the affair and immediately divorced his wife eight years ago. She got her car, her clothes, and her new guy. St. Claire got the house, his car, the money, and everything else. The female judge didn't like women who cheat." He took another bite of his cake donut. "St. Claire's ex also lost her new guy in a couple years. Seems with no money and no brains, the lady didn't have much market value except her looks, which only go so far with most men."

Virginia asked, "Did you find anything about the gold coins?"

Jordan shook his head. "Nothing that isn't already known." He looked hopefully at Virginia and Natalie. "You two do anything besides shooting people?"

CHAPTER 11

Virginia glanced at Natalie, set her donut down, and cleared her throat. "We found out pretty much what you did. But we also located a quilt made by a Seneca Indian woman back in the 1920s who witnessed the robbery of the original thieves." She held up her hand motioning for Deputy Ferguson to hold his question. "The Seneca woman is dead. But she made a quilt that, according to our research, may hold some clues. The woman who presently owns it will be meeting with Natalie and me later today. She has a gentleman with her who may be able to add some information."

Agent Jordan's surprised expression changed to a formal one. "When will we be meeting this woman? How did you find her? What quilt?"

Natalie set her donut down. "That's a lot of questions at once. First, you and the deputy are not meeting her before us or with us. We'll tell you what we learned."

"But—"

"Someone already hired a hit man to kill her and take the quilt. We will be doing this alone."

"I see. I don't like it, but you have the upper hand right now," Agent Jordan said stiffly.

Natalie nodded. "Yes, we do. We aren't being impossible, just cautious."

"We will also be interviewing Mr. Jarvis today," Virginia said.

Jordan turned to Ferguson. "Looks like we sit and wait for these ladies to do the work for us."

Ferguson frowned. "I don't like this. We should be involved with these interviews."

Virginia shook her head. "Like we said before, someone is using Mr. Jarvis to find the gold coins. He also foolishly pulled a gun on me. And maybe that same someone hired a killer to kill our contact with the quilt. We—Natalie and I—will handle it. But we'll share what we learn with you. Then we'll probably have to work closer together."

"Is there anything you need us to do at this point?" asked Deputy Ferguson.

"Yes. Have your people keep this place under surveillance. It might be nice to know who comes and goes… besides us, and where they go."

Jordan and Ferguson nodded. "Okay. We'll have our agents and deputies monitor the coming and goings of the Inn. When do you want to meet again?"

"Give us two days, then call me," said Virginia. "We can meet at someplace of your choosing."

The men nodded. "Okay," Ferguson said. They rose. Natalie walked them to the door. When they left, she turned and walked back to the parlor.

"Who do we interview first?" Natalie asked as she sat. "Jarvis or Victoria Longfellow?"

"You know that FBI agent is going to have us shadowed," Virginia said.

"I figured that."

Virginia sipped some coffee. "We can split up. You take Jarvis, and I'll go see Victoria. But we'll need to shake our tails."

Natalie's face brightened. "I have an idea."

"What?"

"We can have the Smithsonian Central Security Service get the New York State Police to have officers in the area. As soon as we spot the tail, we have the state troopers pull them over and detain them for a few minutes so we can get away."

"Might work. But they have radios and will put out the descriptions of our vehicles. With our luck, some bored traffic cop will see us."

Natalie drank her coffee. "Then how do we get away undetected?"

"Use a boat. They have a few here for use by guests. We sail down to Irondequoit and pick up cars there."

"Might work. Let's have the SCSS arrange for the cars so our FBI friend can't get a trace on our credit cards," Natalie cheerfully suggested.

Virginia sighed. "We'd better move fast. That sheriff's deputy would like nothing better than using a drone to watch this place and us."

"Yeah, but I wouldn't put it past our adversary to use a drone as well. They're getting to be like mosquitos."

Twenty minutes later, Virginia and Natalie released the lines holding the long wooden boat from the Inn's dock. Natalie heard something and looked up. Then she pointed. "That low buzzing sound you hear is from a drone that just cleared the treetops. It may belong to the FBI or sheriff to help watch the Inn."

"Or it's there to follow us. A little obvious for stealth surveillance don't you think?" Virginia slid a rifle out from a leather bag. "I'll take care of that. You start the motor and slowly head out into the lake. I'll jump ashore and wait for it to get closer. Then we'll cost the sheriff's office or someone some bucks."

Natalie tilted her head and stared at the weapon. "Where'd you get that?"

"From the basement of the Inn. It's a World War II M-1 Grand rifle. It's in excellent condition and even had a box of ammunition next to it. Maybe the people who own the Inn like to hunt."

"So, you...borrowed it?"

Virginia nodded. "Yep. I'll put it back later."

"It looks bigger than a .22."

"It's a .30 caliber rifle. The army and marines used them in World War II and Korea. Should easily do the job." She turned toward the buzzing sound. "That's if I can hit it." Virginia hopped out of the boat and dashed for a clump of trees. "Go draw that thing your way."

"Okay." Natalie fiddled with the shift lever, opened the choke, pumped the gas bulb, then yanked the starter cord. The engine coughed, then fell silent. She yanked again, then again. The engine sputtered to life, and Natalie shoved the throttle all the way forward. The engine whined, and the boat surged from the dock and headed out into Lake Ontario.

The drone rose, trying to gain altitude then flew toward Natalie. The buzz of its propeller grew louder. As it passed the old lighthouse and banked toward the lake, Virginia backed against a pine tree, tucked the rifle to her shoulder, aimed at the small, moving target, and fired twice. The drone blew apart and tumbled to the rocks below.

Virginia rubbed her shoulder as she strode back to the dock. She waited for Natalie to bring the boat back, then jumped into it. "I held that rifle tight in my shoulder, but I wasn't expecting that much kick." She slid the gun back into the leather bag and closed it.

"You got it. That was a good shot." Natalie pointed at the Inn above them. "The ladies must have heard the rifle shots. Some are on the balcony. This'll give them something to talk about. Now let's get out of here before our two lawmen friends get more creative." She cranked up the speed and the boat shot out into the smooth lake leaving a creamy wake behind. Greenish tops of jagged underwater rocks, covered with waving seaweed, flashed underneath them.

Ellen stood on the balcony, watching the boat head into the lake before it turned south. She slowly punched a number into her cellphone.

CHAPTER 12

Virginia sat back in her seat as Natalie navigated their way west along the coast to Irondequoit Bay. She slowed and turned under a bridge into the bay.

Virginia looked at her notes from her conversation with Tom at the Smithsonian Central Security Service. She pointed. "That's the marina we're to tie up at."

Natalie turned the boat and proceeded to a small marina. "Doesn't look like much."

Virginia hopped out of the boat when Natalie slipped it alongside a rickety, wooden dock and tied the boat to the pier. She looked around as Natalie picked up the rifle bag and climbed onto the dock.

Natalie studied the area then gave a sideway glance to Virginia. "Okay, where's the welcoming committee?" She hitched the rifle bag higher on her shoulder. "How much does this M-1 thing weigh?"

"About eight and a half pounds." Virginia looked at her watch. "Let's go up to that building and pay for our docking. I'm sure our vehicles will be here shortly."

They marched down the dock, then up a slight slope to a small shack in need of paint. They entered, looked around at the various fishing lures, poles, nets, a live bait tank, and maps on the walls and benches, then strolled to the counter.

A wrinkled, gray-haired man, who Virginia thought must have fought in the Civil War, grimaced as he slowly rose from his chair, set a book down, and smiled. "How can I help you ladies?" He straightened slightly to peer down the slope at the tied up boat. "That your boat?"

Virginia nodded. "Yes, sir. We'd like to pay you to let us keep it here for a few hours. We're waiting for a couple of cars to be delivered here as well."

The old man nodded. "Are you two Special Agents Virginia and Natalie?"

Shocked, they both nodded. Virginia frowned. "Yes, sir. How'd you know who we are?" They fished their credentials and badges from their pockets and showed them to him.

"I was told this morning to expect you. Just leave the boat here. I'll move it to the covered dock just over there. It will be safe." He turned to a wall clock behind them, then looked back at the women. "Your vehicles will be here in a couple minutes."

"How much do we owe you for keeping our little yacht here for the day?"

The old man chuckled. "Yacht huh? Nice joke." He returned to his chair, pulled out a pipe and started to fill it. "It's been taken care of by your agency, very generous by the way." He finished filling the pipe, tapped the tobacco then lit it. He smiled at Virginia and Natalie. "I know there's a no smoking sign but I own this establishment, so I figure I can indulge."

"Yes, sir." Natalie set the rifle bag down. "You know who we work for?"

He nodded. "Yes. The Smithsonian. Never had anyone from there come here." He took a puff and blew the smoke to the side. "Can I give you ladies any directions?"

Virginia shook her head. "We've got directions, all we need now is our cars."

"Should be here momentarily if the gentleman on the phone was right." He tilted his head and listened. "I think your chariots have arrived. They're coming down the hill."

Virginia listened. "I don't hear—okay the driveway is gravel. I hear them now. Sir, your hearing is better than mine."

"Well Miss, my eyesight isn't what it used to be, and my joints ache most of the time, but I can hear good."

Natalie stepped closer and smiled. "What did you do before owning this establishment?"

"Establishment?" He laughed. "Honey, I like you. I was a captain of a ship for years, then retired right after the Gulf War. Family was from here, so I settled in this area. Probably should have gone to Arizona, Texas, or Florida."

"Did you command a cruise ship or a freighter, sir?"

"No. Nothing as glamorous. I commanded the U.S.S. Missouri."

Virginia stiffened. "The battleship? Wow. What an honor to meet you, sir."

"Thank you, Miss." He nodded. "She served valiantly until after that war. Besides her nine 16-inch guns, she was fitted with cruise missiles and all sorts of new electronics and weapons systems. But the Navy decided that she and I were too old and should retire. So, here I am helping a couple of pretty ladies who are also feds."

Virginia heard car doors close and steps in the gravel. "I think our rides finally got here. Thank you for your assistance, sir."

"No problem. You two can stop by anytime."

Virginia and Natalie turned as the shop's door opened and two men in dark suits entered. They stopped at the door, staring at Natalie and Virginia. One took a step closer. "We are looking for Agents Davies and North."

Virginia's lips turned up. "That's us."

The man by the door reached under his coat. The old man stood and brandished a long-barreled revolver. "You'd better be able to eat whatever you're taking from under your jacket young man."

The dark-suited man froze. "I was just getting my cellphone to verify these two ladies' identities."

"Move slow."

"Yes, sir." The man pulled out his phone and punched the screen. He looked at Virginia and Natalie then slid his phone back in his pocket. "Okay. You're good." He swallowed. "I think you can put that cannon away, sir. We're with the same agency as they are."

The old man kept his gun on them. "Prove it. But no quick moves, this here weapon has a hair trigger, and my fingers twitch when I'm nervous."

The men slowly pulled out the badge cases and handed them to Natalie. She examined both, then returned them. "They look authentic."

The old man slid his gun back under the counter. "If you say they're okay, Miss Natalie, that's good enough for me."

The lead suit shook his head and smiled at Virginia. "Looks like you made a good friend."

"Yes," Virginia said, "and don't even think of reporting him for that gun. We'll come after you, and believe me, you two don't want to upset us."

The man closest to the door turned and motioned for them to leave. "That's what Washington said. Okay, ready to go?"

"Are we dropping you two off someplace?" Virginia asked.

"We were told to go with you."

"Sorry, boys. Natalie and I work as a team without outside help unless we ask for it."

"But—"

"Tell you what we'll do. You guys stay here with this nice gentleman and talk about fishing, sports, or your war stories. Natalie and I will be on our way. We should be back in a couple hours. We'll call if we need help." She turned to Natalie and motioned for them to go, then stopped. "Keys in the cars?"

The suit by the door fished two sets of keys from his pocket and handed them to Virginia and Natalie.

The women exited the building and hurried to the cars. Virginia stopped. "Did the Smithsonian tell you where they're keeping Frank Jarvis?"

Natalie nodded. "Yep. Got a text from Tom in Washington earlier."

"Good. Now remember… play nice, and don't hurt him too badly."

"I'll be like his mother," Natalie said as she unbuttoned a couple of buttons on her blouse.

"Somehow I don't think he'll visualize you as his mother."

"Probably right. I'll be on my best… scratch that… I'll use my most convincing behavior."

"That's what worries me. Okay, call me when you're finished. We'll meet back here. Remember you can't waterboard him."

"Don't worry. I'll think of something else."

They drove up the gravel driveway, and Natalie headed into Rochester as Virginia drove to Irondequoit.

Virginia pulled into the narrow driveway of a small, well-kept white house with green trim and a single garage on Queensboro Road in Irondequoit. She climbed out of the car, grabbed her backpack, and headed for the front door. As she approached, the door opened. The man was dark, with black hair and eyes, and skin so bronzed he might have been part Indian. The coppery shade was not restricted to his face and hands; his shirt was open all the way to his belt displaying beautifully rippled muscles. His arms were folded. He looked completely relaxed, except for his face, which was set in an expression of freezing disapproval. Virginia stopped, pulled out her credentials and displayed them, then smiled. "Hello. I'm Special Agent Virginia Davies Clark from the Smithsonian Central Security Service. I have an appointment with Victoria Longfellow and someone named John."

"I'm John. You are expected, Agent Clark. Please come in." As Virginia entered, John leaned out and glanced down the street at a car parked by the curb. "Cars like the one parked down the street have been there since yesterday. We called the police, and they cruise by but don't bother the two men inside. Are they from your agency?"

Virginia entered the living room. "Yes. They're here to protect Victoria, you, and a special quilt."

John nodded. "Please have a seat. I'll get her and the quilt you wanted." He turned and walked through the dining room toward the kitchen as Virginia sat on the couch.

A few minutes later John returned with a woman in her sixties carrying a folded blue quilt. The woman sat on an overstuffed wing chair next to the fireplace across from Virginia. John stood next to her. "I'm Victoria Longfellow. I'm the person you talked to on the phone."

"Ms. Longfellow, my partner and I are investigating the murder of an amateur archaeologist named James St. Claire. It appears his death has something to do with a stash of twenty-dollar gold coins that were stolen in 1923, then disappeared. A stash worth over sixty million dollars today. We have learned that a Seneca Indian woman saw the... the second theft and hid some information relative to our case in a blue lighthouse quilt."

Victoria handed the quilt to John. "Please give this to Agent Clark, John."

He looked down at her. "Are you sure?"

"Yes." Victoria watched John step across the room and hand the quilt to Virginia.

Virginia looked at the quilt. "This is beautiful. The panels with the lighthouses on them work with the quilting stitching and..." She turned the quilt over. "Wow. The quilt work outlines each lighthouse. This is priceless." She set the quilt on the couch next to her. "May I ask how you came to own this quilt?"

Victoria glanced up and smiled at John, who had returned beside her. "The quilt was made by John's grandmother. She liked lighthouses and the old one down the coast of the lake. She told the story about that night and said she hid some secrets in the quilt for safety. But she died before she told anyone what the secrets were. After a while, it became a family legend. No one took it seriously until now."

"You mean until we contacted you?"

"No. Just this morning a woman called and offered me six thousand dollars for it sight unseen. I told her it wasn't for sale. She was quite upset."

Virginia arched a speculative eyebrow. "Did she give you her name?"

"No. After I told her the quilt wasn't for sale, she said she'd get it anyway, and at least this way I would be compensated."

Virginia eyed the quilt next to her. "I'll call Washington and see if I can match that offer."

"That won't be necessary, Agent Clark. You can take it. I only ask that you guard it... and please return it when you are finished and have Mr. St. Claire's killer behind bars." Victoria motioned to John, who put the quilt in a large paper sack.

"Think of it as us borrowing it from you." Virginia picked up the sack and her backpack. "I'll treat it as if it were mine. I'm a quilter and treasure the work and love what goes into these works of art. I assure you, the quilt will be returned to you. " She noticed John had moved to the front window and was looking outside. "What is it, John?"

"The men who were in that car down the street aren't there. Could that be important?"

Virginia stopped, set the paper sack down, and pulled out her phone. She speed-dialed Tom in Washington and inquired about the agents on surveillance duty at Victoria's home. She listened as her fingers tightened on the phone then she disconnected. She looked at John. "The agents haven't checked in on schedule. Not good. Please take Victoria to a safe place. More agents are on the way to find our people and to protect you two. Until they get here, do you have any way to protect her?"

"Yes. I can and will protect her."

"If there's trouble, call me at once, and then call the police." She handed John a business card. "I'd better get going. If there's trouble, it'll most likely follow me." Virginia grabbed the paper sack containing the quilt, and rushed out the door. Gunfire erupted from the short hedge on the left side of the yard.

CHAPTER 13

Natalie drove her car to the address provided by the Smithsonian Central Security Service. She turned onto Genesee Park Blvd and parked on the street in front of what she thought was a century-old, nicely kept two-story house with a large front porch. She checked the address again, shrugged, and exited her car. She grabbed her backpack from the passenger seat and walked up the short walkway to the porch. She glanced around. A school was up a side street behind her. The other old, two-story homes in the area were quiet. She climbed the steps and rang the doorbell.

A tall, muscular man dressed in jeans and a black t-shirt answered the door. "May I help you?"

Natalie pulled out her credentials and showed them to the man. "I'm Special Agent—"

"Natalie North. We've been waiting for you."

Natalie stared up at the tall man. "You have?"

"Yes. Please come in." He stepped aside and waved her inside. "Washington said to expect you."

She stepped into the small vestibule with stairs on the left. She followed the man through another door into a small but nicely decorated living room. She noticed the fireplace on the far side with built-in wooden bookshelves flanking it. "Washington knew I'd be coming?"

"Yes, ma'am. They said your partner likes you doing interrogations. You get results."

"Let's hope this time I live up to my reputation. I can be a little unorthodox."

He smiled. "We were told that, too. We also have your tool kit ready, should you need it."

Natalie gave him an inquisitive look. "My tool kit?"

"The shop tools they said you like to use. I must say that's ingenious."

"Thank you... I think." Natalie glanced around. "Where is Frank Jarvis?"

"This way." The man led Natalie through a small dining room, past a bay window with a seat, and through a large kitchen to a door. Opening it, he proceeded down three steps to a landing and a door leading to the outside. He turned left and marched down the steps to the cellar. He pointed to a self-standing room in the cellar. "There used to be a big coal furnace that was turned into an oil furnace there until sometime in the 50's. That room is soundproof, and he's sitting inside with a black hood over his head."

"Why the hood?"

"He doesn't know where he is, and coupled with the soundproofing, the experience can be unnerving. Thought we'd soften him up for you."

"Good. Thanks. I guess I'll get started. You can record everything can't you?"

"Affirmative."

" Good. That is, unless I signal to stop."

"Okay." He pointed. "The door is right there. We'll be behind the one-way mirror watching in case you need backup."

Natalie strolled to the door, opened it, and entered.

Frank Jarvis sat at a small table bolted to the floor. His hands were chained to the table. He heard someone enter and stiffened. "Who's there? Can you please remove this hood? It's hard to breathe."

Natalie set her backpack on the floor next to the chair across from Frank. Without speaking she walked around the chair and yanked the hood off. "That better, Frank?"

Frank blinked his eyes then frowned upon seeing Natalie. "You!"

"You were expecting the Easter Bunny?" She took the chair across from him. "I see your gunshot wound has been tended to. Wouldn't want you to bleed to death or get an infection."

Frank hurriedly looked around. "I'm glad you're concerned. Now what's going on? Who are these people? Where am I?"

"You are at a secured, and unknown facility being held for interrogation."

Frank's mouth gaped. "An unknown... held for interrogation? I have rights. I want a lawyer. You can't question me."

Natalie took a deep breath. "Wanna bet? You may not even be in the U.S. Right now, you're a nonperson. Anyway, I just need a few simple answers. Shall we get started?"

Frank yanked on the chain and cuffs attached to the table. "I won't answer any questions."

Natalie nodded. "I understand Frank, but if you ever want to go home... you'll be a nice boy and tell me what I want to know."

"Like hell I will!"

Natalie glanced at her watch. "I have a hair appointment I don't want to miss, so let's get started."

"Did you hear me? I'm not talking. I want my lawyer."

Natalie bent down and removed a manila folder from her backpack. She set it on the metal table, opened it, studied the contents, then gave Frank a hard stare. "I understand, Frank, but first let me go through all this, then we can talk about any rights you have." She tapped a piece of paper with her finger. "According to this, you're in deep financial trouble, Frank." Natalie moved a couple of pages around. "And... I see your problem seems to be with a certain gangster in Rochester and his organization. He appears to be a real bad ass. Gambling problem, Frank? You need help."

He frowned. "Where did you get that information?"

"The treasury department, along with some people who are very upset you haven't paid them."

"The... the treasury department?"

"No. I was kidding about them. But there are some... what I would call unsavory characters who want their money and soon or they're going to start breaking bones, yours in particular."

"That's none of your concern."

"Sure it is. It might help explain your actions of late," Natalie said.

"My money worries are not your problem or the problem of the government." He shifted in his seat.

"Frank, according to these files, your bank records, and the other intelligence I see here, you can't pay these gamblers any time soon. You are going to get seriously injured, and the interest rates are steep. Every day you are late makes it harder to pay off. Next, they'll break a few bones, maybe a kneecap, then they'll offer you a way out by either joining their organization and committing crimes... felonies, or provide them with information they desire from time to time. If the police or feds catch you, you could be in prison for a long time." Natalie conspicuously eyed him. "Seeing your nervousness and physical stature, or lack thereof, you'll be someone's girlfriend soon after entering prison. Just remember... don't drop the soap, and don't bend over in the shower." She watched his expressions. *I hit a nerve.* "I can help you."

Frank wrung his hands. "How?"

"I'll make you a one-time offer. You help me, and I'll see what I can do to get your huge financial problem to go away, so you get a new start."

He sat straighter. His eyes widened. "You can do that? A new start far away from here? You can really do that?"

"I'll see what I can do. But you must help me, Frank." Natalie noticed the perspiration on his brow, and his rapid breathing.

Frank fidgeted in his chair. "That might..."

Natalie watched as Frank's eyes rolled back, and then he passed out. She hurried around the table and tried to revive him, then felt for a pulse. She looked at the camera, "Get medics!"

Frank awoke staring at a ceiling with stars on it. He jerked his arms only to find them handcuffed to the metal side railings on the bed. His feet were bound to the foot of the bed. His head ached. He glanced around the small room. A window was near the bed, and the door sat on the opposite wall. In a chair at the foot of the bed sat Natalie.

She rose and stepped to the side of the bed. "I see you rejoined the world, Frank."

"You're still here? What happened?"

"The doctor said you had a serious anxiety attack. Could have killed you. We couldn't have that could we?"

"Ahh... no."

"Good. See? We agree on something. Now about my offer, Frank. Are you going to cooperate, or do I have the guys here drop you off with your... gambling friends? I heard breaking kneecaps and other bones is their specialty and very painful."

"I don't have much choice, do I?"

"Yes." Natalie adjusted her blonde ponytail. "You always have choices; some are not as good as others. Now I need to know what you know about the gold coins, the murder of the archaeologist, and who's paying you to be involved." Natalie wet her lips. "If you owe the gamblers money, then who's paying you and why?" Natalie pulled out a recorder and switched it on. "Go ahead and talk, Frank."

"Okay, okay. I joined a couple guys I know in Rochester to look for the 1923 lost gold coins. You met them at the Inn. They said they had new information about it. I figured if they managed to find the gold, I could get a cut and pay off the gambling debt. Somehow, someone else found out about me. They said the finding of the gold was a long shot, but if we did locate it, and I gave them the information so they could... take it from the guys, they'd make sure my gambling debit got paid, and I could keep my cut of the gold. To sweeten the deal, they paid me to spy on the other two men."

"Who are they?"

"I don't know. Someone from the gambling organization, I guess. They contact me. I can't call or contact them directly. I have an email address. Each time I use it they provide me with a new one to use." Frank shook his head. "I'm desperate and the money was good."

"How did they make the initial payment, Frank?"

"I got a key in the mail to a locker at the Greyhound bus station in Rochester. There was an envelope in it with the cash."

"Good." Natalie gave him a reassuring smile. "How about the murder, Frank?"

"I'm not involved with that. I make a few bucks here and there on the side. Fine. But murder? No way. I don't know anything about that poor archaeologist. I never met him and learned about the murder when you and Mrs. Clark did."

"We're doing fine, Frank." Natalie leaned forward. "Now, who at the Inn is involved besides you, and why?"

Frank wet his lips. "Ellen is doing her best to find the gold coins. She's watching what the guys do."

"Why?"

"I'm not sure. I think there are others involved with her, but I don't know who they are or why she's interested. She's lived there for years... decades really, but now suddenly, she's interested in the gold coins."

"You're doing good, Frank. Now—"

"Ellen knew the murdered archaeologist, James St. Claire. I heard her talking on her phone to someone, and she mentioned it."

Natalie glanced at the recorder, then nodded. "Now this is a new piece of information. Looks like we're going to get along just fine."

Frank swallowed. "I hope so."

"Now why did you draw a gun on Virginia? She shot you. You're lucky she was in a good mood. She could have killed you."

"After all the stuff I mentioned and then the death of that amateur archaeologist, I got frightened. I was so nervous I couldn't think straight. I was terrified. The gun was for my protection. Reaching for the gun when Virginia told me to stop was stupid." Frank looked with teary eyes at Natalie. "I thought I was scared before, but now I'd give anything to be a long way from here. You agreed to get me out of town, right?"

"Yes. But first you're going to work for me. Agreed?"

Frank nodded. "I guess so. Yes."

"Okay. Now remember, you were never here, and you didn't talk to anyone including me."

"That's easy. I don't know where I am."

"You will go back to the Inn and go about your business with the other guys and report everything that happens to me or Virginia. You will keep us informed of what anyone tells you or you see or hear, understand?"

He swallowed. "Okay. But how do I get out of here and back to the Inn, and what do I tell people when they ask where I went and what happened?"

"The nice big gentlemen here who you already met will provide you with an ironclad cover story. And they'll return you to the Inn. No worries. Just don't screw up or panic. Stick to the cover story. Virginia and I will be close and won't let anything happen to you. Remember, we're all on the same side. We'll protect you. Okay?"

"Ye... yes." He looked around. "Looks like I've been given a second chance I probably don't deserve. I'll do as you ask, Agent North."

Natalie switched off the recorder and patted Frank's hand. "You need not have suffered the anxiety attack by just cooperating in the first place."

Frank nodded; his lips turned up in a light smile. "You're right."

Natalie grinned. "Just remember, when you get back to the Inn, if you double cross me, what I'll do to you will make your gambler's threats seem like a day at the beach, okay?"

"Okay. Like you said, we're on the same side."

Natalie stepped to the door, opened it, and called out. "Got what I need, he's all yours, fellas." She glanced over her shoulder. "Have a nice rest of your day, Frank. See you at the Inn." She smiled and disappeared down the hall.

Frank lay in bed shaking. *At least she's pretty and agreed to get me out of this mess and protect me. I hope she's for real. Otherwise, I could end up like the amateur archaeologist.*

CHAPTER 14

Virginia dove off the small front stoop onto the grass as she drew her pistol. She shoved the paper sack with the quilt close behind her and surveilled the hedge. She saw movement. Someone was crouched behind the dense foliage and creeping along toward the street. The person stopped, then rose so his head and his arm holding the gun were exposed. Virginia aimed through the bottom of the hedge at his ankles and fired. He screamed, dropped the gun, and fell to the ground.

Virginia jumped to her feet, grabbed her backpack and the sack, then raced to the spot where the man had fallen. She leaned over the hedge and aimed her pistol at him. He was squirming on the edge of the neighbor's driveway, trying to hold his bleeding and shattered ankle. He glared at her, then continued to swear and scream. As she started to straighten, he reached for his dropped weapon, grabbed it, and turned toward Virginia. She fired four shots. The hollow-point bullets destroyed his arm, elbow, and hand.

Virginia shook her head. "Finished yet? I still have bullets left. Next time I'll put one in your skull." The gun dropped from his bloody hand. Virginia came around the hedge and kicked the gun a few feet away onto the driveway, as he moaned and tried unsuccessfully to stop the bleeding.

A car came screaming around the corner a few houses down the street and rushed toward her. Virginia dropped the paper sack and pressed the magazine eject button, letting the spent magazine drop to the grass. She pulled a new magazine from the side pocket on her backpack, slammed it into the pistol's handle, and racked the slide, inserting a round into the chamber. She aimed at the speeding car. She frowned when she spotted the red and blue lights in the window of the black, unmarked vehicle but kept her finger on the trigger.

The car screeched to a stop. The passenger side door opened, and a man stepped out holding his gold badge up for Virginia. "Don't shoot, Agent Clark. We're from the SCSS."

"Keep your hands where I can see them and step closer," Virginia stated.

The driver came around the front of the vehicle, and with his partner, slowly moved toward Virginia. When they got about fifteen feet in front of her, they stopped. "Our agents on site were attacked after you got here. They got an officer down call out then the radio went silent. They reported that you were in that house they were watching. Someone in one of the houses saw the confrontation and called the local cops."

Virginia held her weapon aimed at them. "Where are our guys now?"

The second agent stated, "A block from here. One agent is getting medical attention for a stab wound, the other one has a small head wound. The medics said they both will be okay. But while we were with them, we heard gunfire in this direction and responded. The Irondequoit police are coming as well. If it'll make you feel better, on the way here, we informed Washington about it and were told to assist you with anything you need by Special Agent Mason."

Virginia lowered her weapon. "Good to know the other agents are going to be okay." She pointed at the now comatose man on the ground in the pool of blood. "I don't need the local cops right now."

"We'll handle it for you. You need to get going on your investigation. If we learn anything from this guy, assuming he survives, we'll inform you." The agent stepped toward the injured man. "You did quite a number on him."

"He shot at me. It pissed me off. I tried to just put him down and neutralize the situation, not kill him. Even then, he tried again. I probably should have shot him in his head the second time."

The two agents chuckled. The driver said, "Probably. But he may already be dead. We'll check him out, call for paramedics, and we'll handle the local LEOs."

Virginia put her gun away. "Why don't we just say local law enforcement organizations instead of LEOs?"

"Television. Mostly NCIS." He listened. "You'd better go, I hear police sirens."

Virginia retrieved the paper sack with the quilt in it. Then she raced back to her car, slid into the driver's seat, tossed her backpack and quilt onto the passenger seat, and fastened her seatbelt. She hurriedly drove down the street and turned the corner as a police car sped by. She drove to the small, rickety marina on Irondequoit Bay. She didn't see Natalie's car. Virginia parked, grabbed her belongings, and rushed into the shack. The agents and the old man were playing cards.

One agent looked up at her. "Agent Clark. Glad you're back. Agent North called, and she's on her way. Traffic is holding her up." He glanced at his watch. "She should be here momentarily."

"Good." She stepped to the table where the men were playing cards. She motioned to the old man. "Can you bring our boat around, please? I'd like for us to leave as soon as possible."

He nodded. "Yes, Miss Virginia. I've already taken these city gents' lunch money." He rose and ambled toward the dock.

Virginia heard a car approach and slide in the gravel to a stop. "Natalie's here."

As they motored the boat along the shoreline, Virginia asked, "How'd the interrogation go?"

"The meeting went great." Natalie told Virginia what Frank had told her and the deal she struck with him.

"When does he get out of the hospital?"

Natalie folded her arms across her chest and frowned. "He didn't need a hospital. I never touched him. I did play some mind games and reasoned with him."

Virginia stared. "Reasoned with him? He's a slime ball. What did you say… join us or I'll ram this huge rusty soldering iron up your rear end or maybe attach certain parts of your body to my car battery and fry them?"

"Nothing so crude. If my reasoning didn't work, maybe… Anyway, I reminded him that he owed a lot of money he doesn't have to some gamblers with no sense of humor, and they'll break his bones one by one if he doesn't pay them soon. So, he either joins us, and we make his problem go away, or he's in for a painful conversation with his gambling associates."

Virginia nodded. "He chose wisely. I take it you ran this by Tom Mason."

Natalie nodded. "Tom reluctantly agreed. The SCSS will also relocate him when this investigation is finished."

"Tom agreed to that, too?"

"He said either he relocates Frank Jarvis, or you and I might relocate him to the bottom of Lake Ontario." Natalie grinned. "He knows us so well."

Natalie noticed the paper sack on the seat next to Virginia. "Is that the lighthouse quilt?"

"Yes. We can examine it in our suite when we get there."

In their suite at the Inn, Virginia spread the blue lighthouse quilt out on her bed. She stood back and said, "It's beautiful. I like the stars and the ship blocks that were sewn, and the use of the lighthouse panels is spectacular. From the blue ribbon attached, it won an award at a quilt show." She turned it over. "Now this is fabulous. Whoever did the quilting made it so each lighthouse is outlined on the back in a field of stars." She pulled a chair up and sat next to the bed then looked at the name block attached to the bottom corner. "This is nice, 'Dave's quilt made with love.' It was made for someone special."

Natalie touched the quilt. "Nice work. Look at that detail." She looked at Virginia. "How'd it go with Victoria Longfellow? Must have gone well if she gave you this quilt."

"Yes, my meeting with Victoria went well. As you can see, she gave me the quilt. But someone either followed us or knew where I'd be. The agents watching Victoria were attacked and when I left the house a man shot at me."

Natalie leaned on the door frame. "Since you're here, I take it the shooter was dispatched to a better world."

"Well, about that. I didn't try to kill him, but he may have bled to death. I'm sure we'll hear if he's alive and says anything." Virginia pointed at the quilt on the bed. "I think we should start to examine this quilt before it gets late. We need to figure out how to hide it as well."

Natalie frowned. "The room could be bugged. So, whatever we do, we'd better do it quietly."

CHAPTER 15

Virginia stepped to the bed and examined the quilt. "I wish my cat was here."

"Leo? Why?" asked Natalie.

"He joins me when I'm working on a quilt or examining one. He'll walk on it, inspect it, ruffle it, and sometimes turns it or folds parts of it, then sleeps on it. When he's done, he has usually found a clue I missed."

"I should have brought your cat and left you home."

"Very funny. Let's take a close look at this." Virginia bent over and studied the quilt, starting at the top. After a half hour of careful examination, she straightened and stretched. "I don't see anything on this side and the back is just a piece of fabric showing the quilting and the outline of the lighthouses. Maybe this is a dead end."

Natalie frowned, shook her head, and said, "Sit and wait a minute. I'll be right back." She started to leave the room when Virginia said, "Where are you going?"

"To get some wine. I have a nice local Chardonnay in my bag."

Virginia plopped onto the bed and sighed. "That may help."

Natalie walked out and came back with the bottle of wine, two glasses and a corkscrew. She opened the bottle, poured out two glasses of the wine and took a sip. "Ahh, the nectar of the gods. Let's hope this pleases the quilting and mystery gods." She sat next to Virginia, and they sipped their wine in silence. After five minutes, Natalie turned and looked at the quilt. "Look at the lighthouse on the right side in the middle."

Virginia turned and squinted at the lighthouse. "What about it?"

"Maybe it's the wine, but to me that lighthouse has something sewn around it, and it looks like the old lighthouse outside before it became a ruin."

Virginia set her wine glass down, walked around the bed, and studied the lighthouse Natalie had pointed to. "You're right. Why didn't I see this before? And it isn't this lighthouse, but you're right; it could have looked like this one."

"I don't know, but take a look. You're the quilt expert, I'm the side-kick."

"I'll be right back." Virginia hurried out of the room and returned with a magnifying glass.

"Where'd you get that?"

"In my backpack."

"Is your backpack your Nancy Drew investigation tool kit?"

"Something like that." Virginia spent the next half hour scrutinizing each lighthouse and scribbling on her notepad. She finally stood and again stretched. "Okay, we may have something."

"What?"

"I'm not sure, but whatever it is, the Seneca woman who made this was very secretive. Now I need a Seneca expert."

"That shouldn't be too hard to find. The Seneca Nation is around here. I'll get my laptop."

"Wait. I know someone who may be able to help."

Natalie raised an eyebrow. "Oh? Who?"

"John, Victoria's friend. It was his grandmother that made the quilt, so he's a Seneca and has heard the stories his grandmother told of the 1929 gold coin robbery and murders."

"Okay. Give him and Victoria a call and make an appointment."

Virginia went to the parlor of their suite and pulled her phone from her backpack. She dialed Victoria's number. After three rings she answered. "Hello?"

"Is this Victoria Longfellow?"

"Yes."

"Ms. Longfellow, this is Special Agent Virginia Davies Clark of the—"

"Smithsonian… police or something. You were just here a while ago and took my quilt to study."

"Yes. We found something in it, but we need some help. I was wondering if we could make an appointment to come to your house and visit with you and John."

"Sure, when?" Victoria answered.

"In about an hour?"

"Better make it two hours. John and I will be waiting."

Virginia smiled. "Okay, my partner and I will be there in two hours."

Natalie strolled out of the bedroom carrying the folded quilt and the bottle of wine. "I take it we're going to see John shortly." She placed the wine bottle on the coffee table. "Better go and get ready. What do you want to do with the quilt? I don't think we should leave it here, especially since Ellen Croft is also interested in it. By the way, what is her involvement?"

"Not completely sure, but we need to keep an eye on her. Just put the quilt in a bag, and we'll keep it with us for now."

"Okay." Natalie headed for her bedroom as Virginia turned towards hers.

An hour later, Virginia and Natalie strolled out of the Inn with their backpacks and the large cloth bag.

Ellen watched them walk to their vehicle, then pulled out her cellphone and dialed a number. When someone answered, she said, "Virginia and Natalie have just left, and they have something in a large bag with them. It may be the quilt we've wanted."

As Virginia drove up the gravel driveway, she felt eyes burning into her back.

CHAPTER 16

Virginia drove along the shore road for a short time, then headed toward Irondequoit. She kept an eye on her rear-view mirror. As they drove through a forest of maples, pine, and oak trees devoid of houses, a car swung in behind her and started to gain on them. Virginia gripped the wheel. "We've got company coming up on us."

Natalie twisted around. "I've seen that car before. It was near the dock where we met that old sailor. Someone tipped these people off again. My money is on Ellen Croft."

"Maybe. Could be almost anyone at this point. We'd better either lose them or stop them."

Natalie tugged on her seatbelt and pulled her revolver out of her back-pack.

Virginia glanced at the large revolver. "You brought that canon? It has just six bullets."

"I have more, and this is my .357 Magnum with hollow point bullets. I can do a lot of damage with it. I only need to hit them once."

"True. I hope you don't have to use it."

Virginia accelerated and raced around corners and down tree-lined straight stretches of road under a shaded canopy of hefty branches and leaves. The other car tried to keep pace but had dropped behind slightly.

Natalie held her phone, "According to Google Maps there is a side road ahead that ends up near Webster, New York. It's about a mile up on the left. We might be able to lose him."

"Okay." Virginia slowed then cut to the left causing the car to sway as she made the turn onto the side road. "The other car is well behind us; I hope he didn't see us turn and this will work."

Natalie pointed ahead. "Pull up into that small clearing between the trees and stop. It's not visible from back there. If they come down here after us, we can stop them and find out what they want, as if I didn't know."

Virginia swung the car into the open area between a stand of dense trees and bushes and aimed the car toward the road. A couple of minutes later the suspect vehicle raced past them. Virginia started forward, then stopped. "If we go back to the main road, they'll probably not catch us."

"According to Goggle Maps, this road winds around then comes out on our road." Natalie chuckled. "I may get to use my .357 after all."

Virginia sighed. "Find another route to where Victoria Longfellow lives. That will save time and possibly reduce the body count."

"Okay." Natalie searched the map on her phone. "Got another route, it's longer but that might be a good thing. In two blocks, turn left. After we see Victoria, let's catch a quick bite for dinner before going back to the Inn."

"Okay." Virginia followed Natalie's directions toward Irondequoit.

Natalie's phone rang. She looked at the screen. "It's Tom from Washington." She answered the call. "Hello, Tom."

"Hello, Natalie, are you with Virginia?"

"Yes."

"Good. Put me on speaker."

"Okay." Natalie switched the speaker on. "You've got both of us. What's up?"

"You two inquired about a man named Graham Weedon. I have some information about him."

Virginia shook her head. "I forgot about that. Glad you followed up."

"We finally located the man. He's in his nineties. Lives in Webster, New York, not far from you. I'll text you his address. His file indicates he has been the subject of numerous police investigations over the decades but managed to avoid arrest and prosecution. Some witnesses died of mysterious causes, others developed amnesia, and others just disappeared. Probably on the bottom of Lake Ontario."

Natalie chuckled. "Nice guy. But with that name I'm guessing he isn't mafia."

"No. But he reportedly was involved in gambling, smuggling, narcotics trafficking, a protection racket, and murder for hire. He has been interested in the gold coins you're searching for as well."

"Is he... has he got all his mental faculties?" Virginia asked.

"Seems so. The word on the street is he's still active, but law enforcement can't seem to put their fingers or handcuffs on him. Oh, one more thing, Mr. Weedon has a daughter that lives there. Her name is Ellen Croft."

CHAPTER 17

After the phone call from their boss Tom in Washington, Virginia shook her head. "We forgot about Mr. Weedon. It's a good thing that Tom didn't."

Natalie sighed. "And who'd have guessed his daughter is Ellen Croft? Now her possible involvement takes on new emphasis on our part. I'll bet she's the leak."

Virginia followed Natalie's instructions from Google Maps and finally entered Irondequoit. As they slowly drove down Queensboro Road, Virginia asked Natalie, "Do you have the pictures we took of the tomahawk at the murder site of the archaeologist?"

"Yeah, they're on my phone. Why?"

"Since we're asking John and Victoria Longfellow about the symbols on the quilt, we can also inquire about the tomahawk. It might have a significance to the murder and our treasure hunt."

Natalie turned on the picture app on her phone and found the photographs of the tomahawk. "Yep, here they are. I took six just to be sure I captured everything."

Virginia parked her car in front of the white two-story house with green trim and a single garage she visited before. "Okay, we're here. Let's see what we can learn then—"

"Go to dinner?" asked Natalie. "I'm getting hungry. Missed lunch." Natalie grabbed her backpack and the bag with the quilt and exited the vehicle.

"Poor baby. Okay, we'll find a place to eat when we're through here."

"Good."

They walked up the short walkway to the small front stoop and rang the doorbell.

A tall man in a dark suit answered the door. "Agents Clark and North, right?"

Virginia slipped her hand into her black leather backpack and gripped her pistol. "Yes."

"I'm Special Agent Abrams, SCSS. I recognize you two from the pictures Washington sent. Please come in." He presented his badge and credentials.

They entered the front room. John and Victoria sat on the couch. Another agent stood in the dining room. Virginia frowned. "Why are the two SCSS agents in here? I saw the car down the street with agents."

"We had another incident. With their permission, Washington had us stationed in here to protect these nice people."

"We need to let you know about a recent development," stated Virginia.

The agent chuckled. "Mr. Weedon?"

Virginia raised an eyebrow. "They informed you?"

"Yes."

Virginia turned to see Natalie sitting next to John, showing him the tomahawk pictures. "I'd better get to work, or she'll take all the credit." Virginia joined Natalie.

John examined the photos on Natalie's phone. "Yes, that is a Seneca ceremonial weapon. That particular one dates from the early part of the 1900s. Where did you find it?"

"At a murder site," stated Natalie.

"Murder? Who was killed?"

"An archaeologist. He was killed at the old dilapidated lighthouse just east of Webster on the coast of the lake."

"I see. I know the place." John rubbed his chin. "I can tell you those stripes and those carvings on the handle are not normal."

Virginia looked at the pictures. "How so?"

"Well, they appear to be part of something else. Like a key to something," John said.

"Key? Hmm. Okay." Virginia pulled her notebook from her backpack, thumbed to the right pages, and showed John and Victoria the images she copied from the lighthouse quilt. "Can you tell us anything about these symbols?"

John looked at the symbols then glanced at Virginia. "These were on the quilt?"

"Yes. We had to work at finding them."

"I bet you did. We've had that quilt for decades and never saw these."

Virginia gave him a hopeful look. "Do you or Victoria have any idea what they mean?"

Victoria nodded. "Yes. Can you show us exactly where on the quilt they were found?"

"Sure." Virginia pulled the folded quilt from the bag and spread it out on the carpet. She pointed at various places on the quilt and to some of the fine quilting around the lighthouses. "The symbols are hard to see."

"I never noticed them before," Victoria said. "The symbols mean the… the treasure is somewhere near the lighthouse. And they indicate the person who stole the treasure from the original thieves and killed them was a Seneca."

John nodded. "This is most disturbing. My people involved in this."

Natalie smiled. "It may have looked like that to your grandmother, but it was dark. Right now, that's not important. That was over a hundred years ago. The location of the treasure, and apprehending the murderer of the archaeologist, are more important."

John gave her a small smile. "Thank you, Agent North. This may help. Our people have said for a century that the treasure was on Seneca land. The symbols on the quilt also indicate that to be the case. My other sister lives near the old lighthouse and yesterday said that some man had been doing some research on the reservation and was killed because he found something related to the old treasure stories."

Virginia frowned. "John, you said other sister?"

"Yes." He touched Victoria's arm and gave her a quick smile. "Victoria is my older sister. Linda is my younger sister."

"Where can we find her? If this gets out, she might be in danger. We can arrange for protection for her."

"Last week, Linda said she was going to some quilting retreat at the Inn near the lighthouse. She said it was convenient."

Natalie started to fold up the quilt. "I remember her from our first night. We'd better get back as fast as possible." She looked at Virginia. "Call the sheriff?"

"No. We need to talk to that deputy and the FBI agent when we return to the Inn. We can either arrange protection or have the deputy do it." She looked at John and Victoria. "Does anyone else know this?"

John bit his lip. "I don't know. But she's friends with the owner of the Inn, Ellen Croft."

CHAPTER 18

Virginia sped through the towns of Irondequoit and Webster to return to the Inn as fast as possible.

Natalie frowned. "I guess this means we have to wait for dinner."

"How can you think about food at a time like this. Linda may be in trouble."

"She's been fine up to now. And Ellen Croft doesn't know we're on to her."

Virginia nodded. "You have a point. We need to provide protection for her but not be obvious."

"At a quilt retreat? This is not going to be easy. Maybe the sheriff has an undercover female deputy that is a quilter who can sign in at the last moment."

Virginia swung the car around a slow driver. "Maybe, but I have an idea."

Natalie shook her head. "Oh, boy, I'm not going to like this, am I?"

"You know me so well. Look, the treasure is possibly close to the Inn and on Seneca land. The murder was there."

"Okay. But what does that have to do with your idea that I'm not going to like?"

"You are going to be Linda's babysitter."

Natalie pouted. "Oh, goodie. I still want to get something to eat. You owe me now. My stomach thinks my throat's been cut." Natalie turned in her seatbelt. "I need nourishment, food, sustenance, libations—"

"Okay, okay, I get it. You're hungry. What do you feel like?"

"A big lobster would be nice," Natalie said with a big grin.

"Guess again," Virginia said.

"A nice juicy steak, sautéed mushrooms, mashed potatoes and... maybe a slice of apple pie?"

"Does her highness have another idea?"

"Humph. A hamburger and fries?" Natalie sighed, then gave Virginia a questioning look. "How about Chinese takeout?"

"Bingo."

Natalie frowned. "Bingo? Hamburgers or Chinese?"

"Chinese. There's a Chinese restaurant a couple miles east of the Inn. Is that an okay bribe?"

"It'll do for now." Natalie looked ahead. "Are we there yet?"

Virginia laughed. "Almost."

Back at the Inn and in their suite, Virginia and Natalie sat at a square wooden table in the dining area eating their Chinese takeout. Virginia set her fork down. "I've been thinking. What if we're looking at this all wrong?"

Natalie finished chewing her piece of sweet and sour pork and asked, "What do you mean?"

"We have been chasing down the quilt, because it has something in it that may have something to do with the treasure."

"Okay."

"But we also have a murder to solve."

Natalie took a bite of her food. "So? We already think they're related."

"Right. We ran checks on the men who found you attractive and you even made one your spy. But so far, the only quilters we've got anything on are Linda and Ellen."

"And we are pretty sure Ellen is after the treasure." Natalie bit into her egg roll.

"But Ellen's involvement doesn't make her guilty of anything other than being a retired mobster's daughter and wanting to find the treasure... at least not yet," Virginia said, then attacked her food. "This is good."

"So, what devious idea is brewing in that head of yours?"

"We get cozy with the ladies, especially Linda and Ellen, you get cozy with your male fan club, and we watch and listen," Virginia stated.

"Why don't we start with that, but you examine the quilt more and find out from Linda what the tomahawk means," Natalie said. "If we can locate the treasure, we'll probably flush out the killer. At least we know Linda is safe in the session on quilt binding going on right now. She's with eight other women."

"Yeah, but we need to keep a close eye on her." Virginia sat back and grinned. "I like it when a plan comes together." She finished her meal.

As they cleaned up their takeout boxes, someone knocked on their door.

Virginia hurried to the door and looked through the peephole. "Oh, boy."

CHAPTER 19

Virginia opened the door and stared at FBI Special Agent Jordan. "Hello, Agent Jordan. To what do we owe this visit?" She stepped aside and motioned for him to enter the room. She closed the door behind her and followed him in.

Natalie finished putting the takeout boxes in the trash and turned. "Well, if it isn't the FBI. Hi."

"Hello, Ms. North." Jordan stood, glancing around the suite.

"Have a seat. What can we do for you?"

"I have some… news." He sat on a green, upholstered chair.

"You found the killer?" Natalie asked.

"No. But Frank Jarvis is dead."

Virginia stepped to his side. "Frank is dead. How did he die?"

"His body washed up on the shore a few miles east of here," Jordan stated. "The coroner said it looks like he drowned. He also said there was a recent gunshot wound that was professionally treated. With that wound, he shouldn't have been trying to swim in the lake. But he'll know more after the autopsy."

Natalie sat on the sofa. "Frank's death will be treated as a suspicious death, right?"

"Deputy Ferguson is treating it as such. He and I thought we should let you know as soon as possible. His body was found a couple hours ago. Ferguson is notifying his next of kin."

"Does Deputy Ferguson have anything to go on?"

Jordan shook his head. "Not much. Frank Jarvis went for a swim this morning. And before you ask, from what we learned from his friends, he went alone." He glanced at Virginia and Natalie. "Have you two got anything?"

Virginia pulled up a chair from the dining table and sat. "We had a lead that said the lighthouse quilt has something in it that may lead to the treasure. And before your people got to the murder site of the archaeologist, we got there and took some pictures of a ceremonial tomahawk. It now seems the markings on it are the key to the information we found on the quilt. We figure if we locate the treasure, that will flush out the killer. I haven't seen much else to go on, so we took this approach. Oh, you do know I shot Frank? He was treated and agreed to help Natalie and me."

"I didn't know. That at least clears up his wound." Jordan rubbed an eyebrow. "Why'd you shoot him?"

"He pulled a gun on me. But I didn't want to kill him. He was treated and after that he agreed to help us."

"When was all this?"

"That's not important. But there is more."

Jordan sighed. "I was afraid of that. Okay, what else do you have?"

Virginia and Natalie told him about the quilt, John, Victoria Longfellow, the retired gangster Graham Weedon and his daughter Ellen Croft, and Linda.

He sat stunned. "You two have been busy. Is there anything else?"

"Yes." Virginia rubbed her hands together. "Someone is behind all this and calling the shots, and we're just starting to peel the onion. We need to talk to Linda Longfellow and protect her. But we need to do it so as not to attract attention."

Jordan eyed Virginia. "I bet you have a plan."

Natalie chuckled. "You're catching on fast. Yes, she does. I'm going to be Linda Longfellow's babysitter, get closer with the other gentlemen here, and get more involved with the quilting. Virginia is going to try and track down the treasure. Then we get the killer and whoever is behind all this to come after us."

"That's dangerous."

Virginia took a breath. "Won't be the first time."

"Okay, what can I do to help?" asked Jordan.

Virginia shifted in her chair. "Find out what the deputy learns about Frank's death. Help me when I go looking for the treasure."

"When will that be?"

"Soon."

He raised an eyebrow. "Soon? Like how soon?"

Virginia wet her lips. "As soon as I get with Linda, and we crack the code on the blue lighthouse quilt. I'm guessing in a day or two."

Jordan smiled. "I'll expect your call and will provide whatever you need."

"It's whatever *we* need, Agent Jordan," Virginia said. "We're all in this together."

Natalie stood. "And if possible, you'll make the arrest."

"Me?"

"You and the deputy. We have a quilt retreat to attend," Natalie said with a gleeful expression.

Jordan glanced around. "Can I ask another question?"

Virginia tilted her head. "Sure. What is it?"

"Where is the quilt now?"

"Safe." Virginia gave him a sexy look. "Oh, do you happen to have a female agent who's a quilter? She may be able to protect Linda Longfellow and free up Natalie."

Jordan's brow furrowed as he thought. "There might be an agent in Buffalo who fits that description. I'll find out. Knowing you two, I assume you needed her yesterday."

Virginia shrugged her shoulder. "That would be nice."

"How would she get in? Isn't the registration for this closed?"

"Leave that to me."

CHAPTER 20

After Agent Jordan left, Virginia went to talk to Ellen Croft about a late attendee. She returned to her room with Linda Longfellow.

Natalie turned from her laptop on the small wooden desk on the far wall, smiled, and rose. "Hi, you must be Linda."

Linda's long, silky, black hair swished as she nodded. "Yes. You must be Natalie North. I've heard the gentlemen here talking about you. They think you're pretty and sexy and are fascinated with you. One of them said you were an actress and a producer in Hollywood ."

"Yeah, that's true, but it doesn't take much to impress them. I'm glad you're here."

Linda looked at Virginia and Natalie. "Virginia said she needed my help. What's going on?"

Virginia pointed to the couch. "Have a seat and we'll bring you up to speed. John and Victoria Longfellow said you are the one who could help us with a case we're working on."

Linda looked confused. "Okay."

"I take it they haven't talked to you about us."

"No. Why would they? What's going on?"

Virginia sat next to her and explained the situation and what they needed from Linda.

Linda sat dumbfounded for a minute, then she said, "You have the ceremonial tomahawk and the lighthouse quilt?"

Natalie held up a finger. "I'll be right back. I'll get the quilt." She headed for her bedroom. She returned holding the large folded blue quilt and a manila folder. "Here's the quilt and the pictures of the Tomahawk we took. It's actually in the possession of the FBI."

Linda bit her lip. "That is unusual."

Virginia gave her a quizzical expression. "How so?"

"This tomahawk is of ceremonial significance to our people. But considering it will lead to the capture of the people responsible for the archeologist's murder, I'll do what I can."

"Thank you."

Natalie spread the quilt out on the floor and laid the photographs next to it. "This is all we've got."

Linda stood and stepped to the quilt, bent down, and examined it. Then she looked at the pictures. "Okay." She pointed at a picture. "These markings indicate we count down three lighthouses and over two from the top." She waved her hand over the quilt then pointed. "That one."

Virginia and Natalie bent over and looked at the lighthouse on the block. "It isn't the old one outside," Virginia stated.

"No. But this lighthouse is the one my ancestor used for the clue."

Virginia looked at the quilt again. "What's the clue?"

"The lighthouse is the starting point on a... well, sort of a map." Linda looked at the pictures again, then picked one up. She frowned as she studied it. "These marks indicate a distance, but it's vague, and... and I'm not sure about this one."

Virginia leaned close and looked at the picture of the tomahawk. Which one?"

Linda pointed at some carvings on the handle of the tomahawk. "These symbols indicate that the treasure or coins are located... that can't be right."

Virginia looked at the photograph of the tomahawk again, then at Linda. "What's wrong?"

Linda frowned. "The treasure is not too far. And these symbols mean... backwards or reversed."

Natalie eyed the photograph. "Backwards? Backwards from what?"

"I don't know," responded Linda.

"How does the quilt fit in?" Virginia asked.

"The quilt has the information you need. It's a map. The tomahawk indicates something about the lake and a... pond or something." Linda pointed. "This means in the direction of the wavy night spirit lights. That's what I don't get."

Virginia returned to her seat and sighed. "The lake and a pond. The reservation. In the direction of the wavy night spirit lights and the quilt is the map." She watched Linda straighten and return to her seat. "What does all that mean?"

Linda shook her head. "I have no idea."

Natalie laughed. "Too bad your cat Leo isn't here to help."

Virginia stared at Natalie then grinned. "Yes, he's exactly what we need." Virginia stood. "Linda, we need to ask you not to say anything about this to anyone. Another quilter will be joining the event shortly and will be your best friend while here."

Linda looked puzzled. "She will? Why?"

"She'll be your bodyguard. She's an FBI agent whose hobby is quilting. She'll be undercover and to anyone here at the retreat, she's just another quilter."

Linda bit her lip. "I need a bodyguard? Am I in some sort of danger?"

"We think so. So far, one of the men from the group you mentioned earlier was murdered. He had an interest in the case. I was attacked at John and Victoria's home by armed men. We have arranged for them to be protected and now we want to keep you safe. I'm sure you will like her."

Linda's lip twitched. "As you can see by what I've told you, I don't know much, but if you think I need a bodyguard, I'll cooperate. If there is nothing else, I must get ready for another class." She forced a smile. "When will I meet this new quilter… bodyguard?"

Virginia rose. "Tomorrow. She'll introduce herself to you."

Linda nodded. "Okay."

Virginia and Natalie showed Linda to the door and then turned back to the quilt on the floor.

Natalie stepped around the quilt and eyed Virginia. "What's going through that devious mind of yours?"

"My cat."

"He's not here. He's probably buying something from Amazon on your computer," Natalie said as she picked up the tomahawk pictures.

"He probably has one of my credit cards, too. But I can do what he does. I'll show you." Virginia tried folding the quilt in various ways, looking for a pattern. Finally, she placed the quilt back on the floor and sat next to it. "That didn't work."

Natalie pondered the quilt for a while then counted on her fingers. "One, the quilt is the map. Two, the treasure is not far. Three, something to do with the lake and a… pond or something involving water. Four, night wavy spirit lights, and finally, backwards." Natalie wrinkled her brow. "We know about the lake. There must be a little cove or bay near here that isn't too far. Night wavy spirit lights and backwards I don't get."

Virginia's eyebrow shot up. "The Northern Lights. Night wavy spirit lines."

"Night wavy… okay, I'll buy that, but backwards?"

Virginia glanced at the quilt. "Hmm, what if…" She gathered up the quilt and hurried to the bathroom. Inside she held it in front of the mirror. Virginia turned it and folded it then shouted, "Bingo!"

Natalie rushed in. "Bingo? You found something."

"Yes, I used my cat's technique and look." Virginia pointed at the mirror. "Backwards."

CHAPTER 21

Natalie stared at the reflection of the folded quilt as Virginia held it in front of the bathroom mirror. She leaned closer to the image then said, "Okay, what am I supposed to see?"

Virginia released her hold on the bottom of the quilt and pointed. "Look here. See the image?"

"I don't see… wait… I see it. " Natalie's eyes sparkled. "That's a map of sorts. Now all we need to do is figure out where the treasure is from this… crude map. I have a road map of this area in my room. Maybe we can use it along with these images to find it. But first, you hold this up while I get my phone and take a picture of it in the mirror."

"Good idea. We can't drag the quilt all over with us."

After Natalie took the picture, Virginia placed the quilt on the bed, then covered it with the heavy red bedspread. They stepped into the parlor, spread the road map on the oval coffee table, and placed Natalie's phone with the picture on it next to the map. Virginia ran her finger over the roadmap, trying to pinpoint the locations depicted on the quilt. Natalie watched her, then stuck her finger on the map. "I think this is the spot."

Virginia wrinkled her brow as she examined the spot where Natalie pointed. "You may be right. I think a road trip is next. We need to see what's there." Hearing a knock on the suite's door, she looked up from the map. "Circle this spot and put it in your backpack for our road trip. I'll see who's at the door."

Virginia padded to the door and looked through the peephole. "Our favorite FBI agent." She swung the door open, "Hello, Agent Jordan. What brings you back here so quickly?" She stepped aside and motioned for him to enter.

Jordan walked into the room and spotted Natalie stuffing the roadmap into her black backpack. "Going somewhere, ladies?"

Virginia stepped to his side and, ignoring his question, said, "You're here because you missed our charming company?"

Jordan chuckled. "Partly. But I wanted you to know FBI Special

Agent Connie Hathaway will be here before breakfast tomorrow. Once she's registered as a quilter for the retreat, she'll couple up with Linda Longfellow. Ms. Longfellow will soon have her bodyguard."

"Great. That's a relief," Virginia said.

He glanced at Natalie standing guard over her backpack on the floor next to her. "What's with the backpack? You have the gold coins in there?"

Natalie took a breath, then said, "Almost."

Jordan tilted his head then smiled as he looked at Virginia. "You found the location of the treasure, didn't you?"

"Take a seat," Virginia said. "We think we've located the place where the treasure may be. But we haven't confirmed it yet. That's where we are going."

"Good work. I'll want to know how you found it but..." Jordan glanced at his watch. "Nuts. It's late and I have an appointment shortly." He shook his head. "Can you believe the FBI schedules these things this late? Oh, well, keep me informed."

"Okay." Virginia escorted Jordan to the door, then returned to Natalie. "From the looks of the map, it would be easier to get to the spot where the treasure should be by boat. We could borrow one from here and get there quicker than driving."

Natalie looked up from her cellphone, then stepped to the window. "There's a thunderstorm coming and it's already raining. The lake has whitecaps. Probably not a good night to be out there in a small boat, especially with lightening. And it's dark."

Virginia heard water streaming from drainpipes. "Yeah, you're right. We'll take the car." Virginia headed for her bedroom. "I'll get my stuff."

Natalie stood, staring out the window. "I have a better idea. Let's go to bed and do this in the morning. The treasure has been missing since the nineteen-twenties, it isn't going anywhere soon. The weather will probably be better, and I won't be as tired."

Virginia paused. "You're tired?"

"Yeah, it's ten o'clock at night." Natalie pointed out the window. "See... dark and... was that lightening?" The thunderclap was immediate and loud. "I guess so, and it struck somewhere close. I'm going to bed." She started to turn then moved closer to the window and peered out. "It looks like the guys we met when we came here are watching our window from that stand of trees below. Why would they do that in this weather?"

Virginia sighed. "In case we venture out they'll try and follow us. Let's go to bed and leave them to enjoy the storm."

"I think I'll slip my gun under my pillow tonight," muttered Natalie.

Jake Thompson tugged his raincoat tighter as he stood in the rain watching Virginia's and Natalie's windows. He wiped the moisture from his face and turned to Jason Ragget. "Looks like the ladies are turning in for the night. We can wait a while, then break in and see what they've got."

Jason shivered. "Not me. I heard from the deputy sheriff that those two are dangerous. Remember, Virginia shot Jarvis when he pulled a gun on her. Let's just keep following them. From the way the FBI agent and the deputy are behaving, I think the women are on to something. Anyway, that lightning strike was close. I'm not becoming a human lightening rod and getting killed for some long-lost treasure. I'm tired, wet, and cold. They're going to bed, and so am I."

With the lights off, Ellen Croft watched the two men from her quilting studio window. *I have a feeling things are going to heat up soon. The cops are jittery, Virginia and Natalie are secretive, and those two are anxious and braving a storm to watch the two women. I'd better make a call.*

CHAPTER 22

The next morning, Virginia and Natalie finished breakfast, then returned to their suite to gather their backpacks, maps, and weapons. Virginia looked out the window. "It's clear and sunny and the lake is calm, so we could take a boat instead of driving."

"Have you seen the weather report?" Natalie asked as she tucked her cellphone in her pocket.

"No."

"According to the weather app on my phone, it'll be nice this morning but clouding up with another storm coming down from Canada by about one this afternoon. I vote for the car."

"Okay, car trip it is. Let's go. Got everything?"

Natalie nodded. "I think so." She hefted the duffle bag that rested on the floor by the couch over her shoulder, then picked up her backpack.

Virginia studied the duffle bag. "Nice purse. Why'd you bring that thing here anyway and why take it now?"

"Do you remember when we were in Italy and that nice CIA guy gave us our toys?"

"Luigi. Yes, I remember. Wait… do you still have some of the weapons he gave us? Are they in there?"

Natalie's face brightened. "Yes. I have what was left after our adventure."

Virginia frowned. "I don't remember you bringing them back with us, and we didn't have trouble with customs, so how'd you manage to smuggle them into the US and get them to Texas without being arrested?"

Natalie leaned against the hall door. "I promised Luigi if he ever came to Texas, I'd go out on a date with him if he could somehow get them to me at my ranch."

Virginia's eyes widened. "You didn't."

"Well, he really wanted a date with you, but I told him you were married. He said he didn't care, married women usually make better dates."

Virginia bristled. "He said that? The pig."

"Not to worry, I convinced him it would be better to go out with me."

Virginia arched a speculative eyebrow "Oh. What were you wearing?"

Natalie gave a mischievous smile. "A thin, tight, black top with a short skirt."

"Of course, you wore it with a black bra or—"

"No. Nothing. And yes, it was see-through. But I had on more fabric than some of my costumes when I was an actress."

"No wonder he was willing to do anything you asked."

"He got over being disappointed from not dating you pretty fast."

Virginia chuckled. "I bet."

"A nice young air force officer delivered a sealed wooden crate to my ranch a week after we got back. It had all sorts of numbers and writing on it and something about a pouch. But our remaining weapons were packaged inside."

"It was a diplomatic pouch, I think. But good for you. Who knows? We might need them."

Natalie shifted the weight on her shoulder. "Can we go now? This is heavy."

After stowing their gear in the car, Virginia slipped behind the wheel. Natalie climbed into the front passenger seat and organized her maps. They fastened their seatbelts and drove up the gravel driveway toward the road, with stones pinging on the undercarriage. "Since the men from the event center watched our rooms last night, and they were inquisitive this morning at breakfast, I have a feeling they'll try tailing us today."

"Yeah, you're probably right. They hurried through breakfast when we said we were going out." Natalie peered at her map. "Turn left at the road and head east."

Virginia turned east on the road, then asked Natalie, "While we drive, will you call Tom at the Smithsonian Central Security Service and ask him to pull Ellen Croft's phone records for this week?"

"Yes. I'll do it now. Just drive for three miles, then there should be a road of sorts on the left. Turn there."

Virginia gave Natalie a quizzical look. "A road of sorts?"

"According to this map, it probably isn't much more than a dirt road or one with a minimal amount of asphalt."

As Virginia drove the last mile or so, storm clouds gathered like a large spreading bruise across the sky. A grey pall cast itself across the land around her. A stray bolt of lightning wouldn't have surprised her. "I think your weather report was a tad off. This storm is ahead of schedule. And we have a tail."

"I bet it's the boys from last night," stated Natalie. "Are you going to shake them?"

"In a manner of speaking. There's no one else around. Do you have some of those small EMPs in your duffle bag left over from Italy?" The EMPs were Electromagnetic Pulse devices that would fry any electrical circuit within a certain radius.

"I think so. I'll take a quick look." Natalie released her seat belt, turned around and rustled through her bag. "Yep. I've got four."

"Get one, and we'll disable their vehicle," Virginia said.

"Yeah, that and any electronic device that's turned on with microchips inside, like cellphones and radios." Natalie pulled one of the small black devices from the bag and turned around. After re-buckling her seat belt, she rolled down her window. "When I toss this, you'd better speed up, so we're out of range."

"I know, it'll cause them to speed up, too, and they'll be almost on top of it when it fires. Ready?"

Virginia hit the accelerator and shot forward. Natalie pressed the start button, then tossed the small device out the window to the side of the road. They watched in the mirrors as the car following sped up to keep pace with Virginia when it suddenly slowed and pulled to the side of the highway.

Natalie did a little dance in her seat. "That was fun. They'll be hard pressed to figure out what happened."

"I don't remember how long that mini-EMP toy of ours stays active, do you?"

"I think Luigi said three minutes. That way, by the time help comes, it'll be dead and look like road trash. But anyone else driving by in the meantime is in for a surprise." Natalie pointed to a shady spot between the towering trees, "Turn up there on the left."

"That's a muddy dirt road."

"You worried about getting the car dirty?"

Virginia sighed. "No." She slowed the car and turned down a rutted, mucky road between stands of maple, oak, and birch trees forming a shaded canopy of hefty branches and leaves.

Natalie eyed her map as the car navigated the ruts and rocks in the road. "This so-called road ends at the lake. With our tail safely stalled behind us, we should have time to explore the area."

"Are there any buildings down this... road?" Virginia asked.

"I don't know. I'll check Goggle maps." Natalie fiddled with her cellphone then leaned forward peering through the front window. "According to this, there should be three structures ahead." She sat back and busied herself with the phone then shook her head. "We're on the Seneca Reservation."

"That's okay, we're feds."

"That smudged sign we just passed said this is posted land and—" The right front tire exploded, followed by the sound of a gunshot.

CHAPTER 23

"Shit," Virginia said, as she stopped the car and shut off the engine. "Now we have another problem. Get out of the car and come around to my side." She pointed toward a small rise. "The shot came from up there."

Natalie unbuckled her seat belt and hopped out, grabbing her backpack and duffle bag. She hurried through ankle-deep mud around the vehicle and joined Virginia. "Okay. Now what?"

"We wait. Someone wanted to stop us, not kill us. I'm pretty sure they'll come down and see who we are."

Natalie sighed. "It's the 'pretty sure' part that bothers me."

After a couple of tense minutes, there was a rustle in the foliage and two men with rifles stepped out of the forest and underbrush. One, wearing a blue rain parka, looked at the car, then the women. "This is posted land. Can't you read? No trespassers. You need to leave."

Virginia pulled her badge case out and displayed her gold SCSS badge and credentials to the men. "We're Special Agents Clark and North. We're federal agents on official business. We can be on this land."

The man stiffened. "Do you have a warrant?"

"We are not here to arrest anyone. We're investigating the murder of an archeologist on the reservation."

The men glanced at each other. "Okay. Sorry about the tire. We get a lot of sightseers, fishermen, and drug people trying to use this area. The local cops are no help, and the tribal police do what they can. You can go ahead; we will not interfere with what you're doing."

Natalie stepped forward, "You shot our tire, so you can change it. The spare is in the back."

The second man looked at the car. "It's muddy."

"Yep, and we're not dirtying our nails doing it. You shot it… you change it."

"You can call triple A," said the second man.

Virginia pulled her 9mm handgun and aimed it at the man. "You shot at federal agents, now put your rifles down and change the damn tire...

now!"

"We didn't know you were federal agents."

"Tough. Lower your weapons."

The man with the parka said, "They'll get—"

Virginia fired a shot into a nearby tree. "I just wounded an innocent tree. Next, it will be you."

Natalie grinned. "You do realize, gentlemen, that she is not kidding? She gets grumpy when her blood sugar gets low, and that is about now. So, I'd do as the lady says."

"But you're special agents. You can't shoot us."

Natalie chuckled. "We're very special. They call us when everyone else strikes out. So, we get a LOT of leeway and special considerations. Considerations meaning, we get away with things others don't. Now lower your weapons and change the tire before she shoots you. If I have to change it and break a nail, I'll be sure to hurt you more than her before you painfully depart this earth. And trust me, no one will find your bodies."

"Okay, we get it." The men held up their hands in surrender, sighed, leaned their rifles against a tree, then got to work changing the tire.

Virginia leaned on a maple tree and smiled as she watched the men working in the mud. "Fellas, I have a couple questions I'd like answers to."

The second man, wearing a sweatshirt, glanced at her and the gun in her hand. "What do you want to know?"

"Did anyone tip you off that we might be coming?"

"Ahh… yeah. We got a call this morning that someone might be coming this way and to discourage them… you."

"Who was it from?"

"Don't know. We were given the message by one of our people. We didn't actually take the call."

"Why is this area so sensitive to your people?"

"It isn't." He stood wiping his dirty hands on his jeans. "This is just an access and fire road down to the lake."

Virginia nodded. "Has anyone else taken an interest in this area lately?"

The first man stood and released the jack. The car settled onto the spare tire. "That's done. Chuck, put the flat tire, jack, and tools back in the trunk." He turned toward Virginia and Natalie. "No one until the call this morning. Now that I think about it, that seems strange."

Natalie rested her foot on the duffle bag sitting on leaves. "Why is that strange?"

"Well, no one has cared about this area in a long time. And the message we were given said a group from the Seneca Nation will be along later to look this area over." He examined the car. "It's fixed. Can we get our rifles now and go?"

Virginia nodded. "Thank you for being gentlemen and volunteering to change the tire, and the information, fellas. Maybe we'll see you later."

"No offense Agent Clark, but we'd rather not see either of you ever again."

"I understand. Have a nice day." She watched them disappear into the forest.

Natalie tossed her duffle bag and backpack into the car and slid into her seat. As Virginia got in, Natalie chuckled, "After how nice we were to them they don't want to see us again? How rude."

"Would you want to see us again?" Virginia asked.

"No, especially with you shooting trees."

Virginia started the car. "Now to see what's down here. Open our makeshift map from the quilt."

"Okay." Natalie fished their map drawing from her backpack and unfolded it. "It looks like we go ahead to a… a cross path or road or something. Once we get there, we can check our bearings."

"We need to be careful of what we do. We don't want to give anything away that we may find. My guess is they'll watch us and report to whomever told them we were coming."

"They lied?"

"I think so."

"Why?"

"I said we were investigating a murder. Everyone knows where it took place, and it isn't here. So why are we out here? They never asked that."

"You're right."

"And the men said others would be along later, after we did our thing. Why, if this area hasn't been all that interesting in a long time?" Virginia pointed ahead. "That must be your crossroad."

"It is." Natalie peered through the window. "Is that a tomahawk in that tree by the intersection, such as it is?"

Virginia nodded. "Yes."

"Why do I wish I'd stayed in bed?"

CHAPTER 24

Virginia pulled to a stop. Natalie hopped out of the car and worked the tomahawk out of the tree and returned to the vehicle with it. Once inside she handed it to Virginia.

Virginia examined it. "It's all black. Why? Is this a message? Maybe it's someone's way of saying go home."

Natalie took the tomahawk back and examined it. "The color must have some significance. Maybe it's a marker of some kind for the others who are coming. Other than the color, I don't see anything outstanding on it."

"Me either. I have an idea," Virginia said.

"Oh, boy. I'd better not break a nail."

"No, you shouldn't break a nail. I was thinking that the tree where you pulled this out of may be part of it, like a direction indicator. So, let's put it into that tree across the intersection. If the tree was important, then whoever is coming may get the wrong directions."

"Can't hurt to try, but why do I have to put it back?"

Virginia smiled, "Your seatbelt is undone."

"Nuts." Natalie climbed out of the car again, looked around, then scurried to the tree across the rutted road. She slammed the tomahawk deep into the trunk of the large tree and returned to the car. "Okay, that's done."

"You put that blade deep into that poor tree. They'll have a hell of a time getting it out."

"Tough." Natalie buckled her seatbelt and picked up her makeshift quilt map. "Turn left here. This road winds down to the lake, but there may be some structures closer to the water."

Virginia turned left—onto what looked more like a muddy path than a road—and slowly cruised around corners, bushes, and tall, thick trees. She drove up a small grade, then at the top she maneuvered around a dead tree lying partway across the path. She spotted the lake ahead and stopped. "So far, besides being shot at and finding a mysterious tomahawk, this trip has been uninspiring."

"Don't forget the tree you shot."

"That wasn't inspiring."

"No, but it was effective."

Virginia sat back. "Now what does that map say?"

Natalie held up the paper with the map and squinted. "I wish I wasn't in a hurry when I copied this stuff. I'm having difficulty reading my writing. Okay… something about a head marks the spot."

"A head marks the spot?" Virginia eyed her skeptically. "Are you kidding?"

"No." Natalie leaned forward peering out the windshield and pointed. "The spot we want should be right up there."

"Let's walk. Maybe something will pop out if we're not driving."

"I hope not," Natalie said as she climbed out of the car. She slid her backpack on, grabbed her duffle bag and joined Virginia in front of their vehicle.

Virginia adjusted the straps on her black backpack and started to hike up the muddy road toward the lake, with Natalie a couple feet behind her.

After a five-minute walk, Natalie called out, "Stop. We should be at our destination."

Virginia glanced around. "I don't see a head."

"It's not going to be on a road sign. We need to hunt for it."

"If you say so. Start looking. A head? Like a shrunken one?"

"I don't know. A head is all I've got."

Virginia looked skeptical but kicked leaves in front of her as she walked around.

Natalie examined tree trunks and boulders in the area. Finally, she sat on a fallen log to rest. Just as she pulled a bottle of water out of her backpack, Virginia yelled as she tripped and fell. Natalie rushed to Virginia, who was cussing at a stone and holding her ankle.

Kneeling, Natalie looked at and probed Virginia's swelling ankle. "You might have sprained it. Doesn't feel like it's broken."

Through clenched teeth, Virginia said, "It hurts like hell."

"I've got bandages and pain drugs in the duffle bag. We'll immobilize it as best we can and give you the pain meds, then get you to a doctor." Natalie glanced around. "What did you trip on?"

Virginia nodded toward a clump of leaves. "There's a rock under those leaves. Of course, I found it the hard way."

Natalie rose and stepped to the leaves. With her foot, she moved the leaves around, exposing the rocks. She bent down and examined it, then rubbed her hand across the flat top surface. She turned and grabbed a small bottle of water from her backpack and poured it on the rock. "Well, well, your sprained ankle might be worth the pain after all. Here's a flat rock with something carved in it. It's a little crude and needed the water to bring it out so as not to be obvious to the casual hiker, but here it is anyway."

Virginia pointed at the wet surface. "What's that?"

"I don't know," Natalie knelt and rubbed more water on the figure in the stone. "It looks like a disembodied head with wings and a column with wavy lines coming from the top. The head looks like it's straight from a horror movie."

"I never thought we'd actually find a rock with a head carved on it. Take a picture of it and the head, we can send it to the Smithsonian later or I'll send it to Dr. Terry Sorenson at my museum to figure out if it's significant."

"Wasn't something like this on the tomahawk blade?" Natalie cleared more leaves. "If so, why didn't someone tell us about it?"

"Put the leaves back. We need to get out of here and obtain help to go any farther. And I need your drugs. As to the flying head, maybe they didn't think it important." Virginia felt her ankle. "Man, this hurts."

Natalie quickly recovered the rocks, gave Virginia the medication, then bandaged her ankle. "Okay, give me the keys. You can't drive."

Virginia fished the car keys from her pocket and gave them to Natalie. "Help me up."

Natalie grabbed her duffle bag and assisted Virginia in standing. She led Virginia to the vehicle and got her into the passenger seat. Natalie hurried around the car and set the duffle bag down, then put her backpack into the car. As she bent down to grab the handle of the duffle bag, a bullet passed over her head and smashed the car's side mirror. *Not again. Don't these people have anything better to do?* Natalie dropped to the ground. She unzipped the bag.

Virginia ducked and scooted across the seat to the open door. "The shooter is near that burned out cabin up on the hill. You can see part of it between the trees. This shooting thing has got to stop." She painfully slid out of the car.

Natalie rummaged around in the bag and pulled out a short, black launcher and a small rocket. She jammed the projectile into the launcher and turned a switch, causing a low hum.

"Give me that. I'm not in the mood to play games," Virginia said. Natalie nodded and handed the mini-RPG (Rocket Propelled Grenade) system to Virginia. She slid to the front of the car as the shooter fired another round at the car. With Natalie's help, Virginia popped up over the hood, quickly aimed, fired, and ducked back down. The rocket shot out of the launcher and raced between the trees toward its target. A couple of seconds later the remains of the burnt-out cabin were obliterated in a fireball. The explosion was thunderous.

Natalie watched as the fireball dissipated and the debris was thrown hundreds of feet. "That'll teach them not to screw with us."

Virginia chuckled. "I think it's time to blow this popsicle stand."

"You just did."

"You know what I mean." Virginia handed the launcher back to Natalie. "We're going to get company soon. That explosion won't go unnoticed."

"Yeah, and the Senecas know we're here. So, let's drive up there and see what's left and if there are any human remains. I'll drive while you call 911," Natalie said.

"Okay. We're just innocent bystanders and federal agents."

"You're devious. But I like it." Natalie helped Virginia back into the car, put the duffle bag in the trunk, found the slightly overgrown path, then carefully drove up the hill to the cabin. "Looks like someone recently drove on this path."

"Maybe the shooter. I wonder if he escaped."

Natalie pulled up in front of the demolished structure and stared. "Houston, we have a problem."

CHAPTER 25

Virginia stared out the front window of the vehicle at the smoldering remains of the old cabin. A smoldering, battered pickup truck with windows blown out rested at an angle against a large rock. She sighed. "Oh, boy. Does the charred truck door look like it has or had a logo on it?"

Natalie nodded. "Yep."

"Tell me it doesn't say Tribal Police."

"Sorry. No can do. We just blew up a cop and his vehicle. I'm surprised it didn't explode even more."

"Me, too. Anyway, He shouldn't have shot at us," Virginia said in a huff. "I wonder where he or she is?"

"Probably all over the place. That was an RPG we shot."

"Yeah. That RPG may have been a little overkill."

Natalie chuckled. "Now you think of that. Want to look around?"

"Probably won't find much now. Anyway, if we don't vamoose, we'll have a lot of explaining to do."

Natalie twisted in her seatbelt and looked at Virginia. "Didn't you call the FBI or the sheriff?"

"No. I forgot. Whatever you gave me for the pain is working and my mind is foggy."

"Okay, we're out of here." Natalie backed up, turned around and drove as fast as was safe down the rutted dirt path. When she reached the crossroad, she turned toward the lake and bounced down toward the water.

Virginia frowned. "Where are you going? The highway is the other direction."

"So are the police or anyone responding to the sound of the RPG and truck explosion. Notice the smoke? According to my crude map, there's a beachfront road or something resembling a road down there. I think we can get out that way."

"I hope you're right. We need to get back to the Inn."

"No, you need a doctor. You're hurt. It's the hospital first."

Four hours later, Virginia and Natalie arrived back at the Inn. Natalie helped Virginia with her crutches and followed her into the Inn and their suite.

Virginia plopped down on the sofa and grinned. "So much for being an ankle sprain."

"Yeah. I was so sure it wasn't broken. Sorry." Natalie eyed Virginia. "The pain drugs have you sounding funny."

"Great, broken ankle and can't think or talk straight. Anyway, that's okay. You got me to the hospital despite my arguments. That's what was important." Virginia's cellphone rang. "Will you grab that for me? I shouldn't have dropped my backpack by the door."

Natalie picked up the pack and pulled out the phone. "Virginia Davies Clark's phone. This is Natalie."

"Hi, Natalie. This is Terry Sorenson from the Georgetown Museum. Virginia called with a request for information. I wanted to get back to her as soon as I could."

"Hi, Terry. Hang on." Natalie stepped to Virginia but said into the phone before handing it to her, "She's high on painkillers right now, so don't worry if she sounds strange."

"Okay, but why? Did she get hurt? How?"

"Yeah. She tripped on a rock and broke her ankle. Here's Virginia." Natalie handed the phone to Virginia.

"Hello, Terry," said Virginia in a slurred voice.

"Okay. What happened?"

"Like Natalie said, I tripped on a rock and fell. Now to business, since you called here, I take it you have some information for me."

"Be more careful, girl. Yes, I've got something. Based on the pictures you sent me and your location, that flying head symbol is that of *Dagwa-noeient*. It's the flying head spirit of the Seneca. He's a monster god of sorts in the form of a giant, ugly, disembodied head, usually created during a particularly violent murder."

Virginia sat up straight. "It's created during a particularly violent murder?"

"According to the legend and their religion, yes."

"Would any Seneca know about this?"

"I don't know. Maybe, especially if they were a big shot in the tribe, a religious figure, or an old person." Virginia heard paper shuffling. "Where did you come across it?"

"On a tomahawk and a rock."

"The rock you tripped on?" Terry asked.

"Yes." Virginia raised her injured, booted foot and rested it on the coffee table in front of her.

"How about the tomahawk?"

"A murdered archeologist had it."

"Hmm. Okay, did the rock have anything else on it?"

"A carving of a column with lines coming from the top."

"Like a lighthouse?" Terry asked.

"Yeah, I hadn't thought of that."

"If you're on strong pain meds, you probably wouldn't."

Virginia sighed. "You're right."

"This could mean whatever you are looking for was involved with a serious murder and is in or near a lighthouse."

"Okay. Thanks, Terry. That's exactly what we needed."

"No problem. If you need anything else, just ask. Oh, and be careful. Someone, most likely a Seneca, is dangerous. You're probably being watched."

CHAPTER 26

Virginia disconnected, rested her phone next to her, and eyed Natalie pouring drinks for them. "What are you doing?"

"Getting some wine for me and some grape juice for you. What did Terry say?"

"Grape juice? I want some wine."

"You are on pain meds. No alcohol. You know you can't have any."

"I know." Virginia ran her fingers through her hair. "Okay. Grape juice, but put it in a wine glass so I can at least pretend it's wine."

Natalie returned to the couch and handed Virginia her juice. "Now, what did Terry have to say?"

"Terry said the horrible symbol is that of *Dagwanoeient.* It's the flying head spirit of the Seneca."

"What does it even mean? Why would it be there?"

"He's a monster god of sorts in the form of a giant, ugly, disembodied head, usually created during a particularly violent murder." Virginia took a sip of her juice. "Maybe the person who carved it saw the mass murder at the lighthouse when the gold was stolen from the original thieves."

"I wonder if it was the Seneca woman who made the quilt. She may have also witnessed where the killer went with the gold coins. That would explain the images and the quilt."

"Yes. And the rectangle with the lines coming from the top may be a lighthouse."

"Terry figured this all out without being here, and we didn't? We're slipping."

"Terry is an archeologist and anthropologist. She's good at this stuff."

Natalie sat back, sipped her wine, and said, "Okay. From what she said and what's been in front of us all this time, I assume we need to locate the... the *Dagwanoeient* head figure at the old lighthouse. But why did our information lead us to the rock by the lake?"

"Maybe that's where the killer took the treasure originally until the heat died down, then moved it. Someone was watching and left a trail for others to follow."

"That seems like a lot of work."

"Moving the treasure to the old lighthouse would make it easier to access." Virginia finished her grape juice.

Natalie took a sip of her wine. "Why didn't you ask our Seneca contacts for the information instead of Terry?"

"Terry, I trust."

"Oh. Okay. What's next? You're kind of sidelined with that foot."

"We recruit help, but I'm still going along to go looking for the treasure. We'll need to be careful. News of our discovery could leak before we want it to."

"Leak to who?"

"The murderer of the amateur archeologist and the people after the treasure. Like I told the FBI agent, once we locate the treasure, we'll flush out the murderer of the archeologist."

"Any idea as to who that might be?"

Virginia nodded. "Yes." She eyed her glass. "Got any more of this juice?"

CHAPTER 27

After breakfast the next morning, Virginia and Natalie walked along the shore of Lake Ontario. Virginia wore a red, loose, untucked blouse, denim shorts, her support boot for her broken ankle, and her crutches. Natalie wore a green untucked blouse and red shorts. When they heard their names being called from the patio of the Inn, Virginia sighed. "I bet that's our FBI friend who wants to talk about some unfortunate incident on the reservation not far from here."

Natalie grinned. "The incident we have no knowledge of but heard an explosion?"

"That's the one." Virginia, limping, led them back to the Inn. They pulled up a pair of green painted, wooden Adirondack chairs and sat facing the lake.

FBI Special Agent Jordan stormed onto the patio and marched in front of the women. In a forceful voice, he said, "I need to talk to you two."

They stared at him.

"Well... aren't you going to ask why, or should I take your silence as admission of the crime?"

Natalie leaned forward and smiled. "What crime?"

Special Agent Jordan balled his hands into fists, face flushed. "The shooting of a tribal policeman and the burning of a building on the reservation. I know you were there."

Virginia looked at her nails then at Jordan. "We were on the reservation yesterday, but what evidence do you have of us shooting anything?"

He gritted his teeth. "I know you were responsible."

"How? And please get something to drink and relax. Your blood pressure will give you a stroke."

He swallowed. His body was stiff and tense. "I... I know you two were on the reservation about the time the call came in at the sheriff's station. The sheriff and the tribal police immediately blocked all access routes as deputies, tribal officers, and the fire department responded."

"I see. And did they find us there?" Virginia asked.

"You know darn well they didn't. Somehow, you two disappeared."

"So, you know we were there, and somehow we escaped the combined best efforts of the sheriff and the tribal police attempting to stop anyone from escaping."

"Ahh… yes… I want to know if you did it, and how you managed to get away."

Natalie leaned back. "What was the tribal officer shot with? A 9mm? .38? .380? .357 magnum? BB gun? Squirt gun?"

Jordan frowned. "Squirt gun? No. From what remained at the site, it looked like some kind of a rocket. Maybe a special kind of RPG."

Natalie tilted her head. "Not a normal RPG?"

"According to my people, no."

"And where would we get an RPG, much less some special one?" Natalie asked.

He turned and glanced at the lake then back at Virginia and Natalie. He took a couple deep breaths. "I don't know where you two could get an RPG of this unique type. Do you?"

"Did you find the body of the tribal policeman at that explosion site yesterday?" Natalie asked.

"Actually, no."

"You don't have any human remains?"

"No."

"What makes you think there was a cop there?" asked Natalie.

"His truck was there. People said he was patrolling the area."

"Is he missing?"

Jordan frowned. "I didn't ask. They said he was patrolling the area, and then we found the burned truck."

"So, all you've got is a blown-up truck, a possible missing cop, and a burned old cabin. No body and no remains. Doesn't sound like anyone was killed or injured." Virginia looked at Natalie, then at Jordan. "If you think you can pin this on us, then arrest us or go away."

Jordan leaned on the side of a close picnic table. "You're not going to cooperate?"

"Do we look stupid?"

Jordan sighed and sat on the table. "Okay. I'm sorry. This explosion and… and possibly killing a tribal officer are serious. I had information from an eyewitness that said you two were on the reservation and the only ones."

Sunlight glistened off the surface of Lake Ontario as Natalie raised an eyebrow. "An eyewitness saw us shoot that nonexistent cop?"

"No. Just that you two were the only people on that part of the reservation."

"Then you've got a problem. If we were the only ones on site, then how could you have an eyewitness who was also there tell you we were the only ones there? Maybe they shot the... special RPG."

"I ahh—"

Virginia grinned. "You don't have a body. You have a truck that was blown up by some mysterious rocket, fired by some unknown assailant, that mysteriously got away. And that's it?"

Jordan sighed, looked at the ground, then at the women. "Yes. My boss said you two were good and also dangerous. I think maybe I let the dangerous part get the best of me."

Virginia casually looked at the small ripples of water lapping the shoreline. "Special Agent Jordan, would you like to know where the old treasure is and who's responsible for the death of local historian and amateur archaeologist, James St. Claire?"

Jordan sat stunned. His face went blank. He stammered, "You... you... you know where the gold coins are and who killed James St. Claire?"

Natalie nodded. "We do."

Jordan hopped off the picnic table and strolled toward the woman. "You actually know who murdered the amateur archaeologist?"

Virginia laughed. "Nice save, Special Agent. Yes, but now we need to prove it. My idea is to go after the gold coins and have the killer try to take them from us."

"You think the murder and the coins are related? Okay, how did you figure that out?"

"The killer knew James St. Claire was researching the old treasure story and found a clue on the reservation. Unfortunately, the murderer struck and managed to kill St. Claire before he divulged any information. The killer didn't have any idea of what St. Claire found."

"But you found what St. Claire had, plus you got more clues from somewhere, you put all that together and found the location of the coins. I take it you found or saw something no one else did."

Virginia tilted her head and looked at him with a sparkle in her eyes. "Bingo!"

CHAPTER 28

Jordan pulled up a red Adirondack chair in front of Virginia and Natalie. He stared at Virginia's foot. "What happened to your foot?"

Virginia gave him a crooked smile. "You noticed. Nothing gets by the FBI, does it?" She glanced at the boot. "I broke my ankle when I tripped on a rock."

"On the reservation?"

"If you must know, yes," Virginia said.

He nodded. "I hope it heals okay. Does it still hurt?"

"Some. The hospital doc gave me a prescription for some pain killers. The only problem is, if I take them, I can't have any wine. It's a difficult dilemma."

Jordan laughed. "I'm sure you'll come to some satisfactory solution." He glanced around. "Okay, what do we do first to locate the treasure, and who's behind all this?"

Natalie chuckled. "To quote Tonto in the old Lone Ranger Movies… 'What do you mean *we*, paleface?'"

Jordan gave her a quizzical look. "Huh?"

Virginia laughed. "She's teasing you. She's not sure the FBI is needed right now."

"Oh." He turned to Natalie. "You two have been on your own for this entire investigation and left me and the sheriff out of the loop. I'm in on this now, so get used to my company." He turned toward Virginia. "What's *our* next move?"

"I like a man who takes charge, or at least tries to. Okay, you're part of the team, but you take orders from me."

He took a breath and slowly let it out. "Considering what you two have accomplished in a short period of time, I'll have to agree or get left out in the cold."

Virginia reached down and rubbed her boot. "I'm glad you see it like that."

Jordan looked at the two women. "Where do we start?"

Virginia turned to Natalie. "Can I have my pills? My ankle is talking to me."

"It's either your meds or wine," Natalie responded.

Virginia eyed her foot. "The pills. I'll have to settle for your nonalcoholic grape juice instead of wine."

"Okay." Natalie opened a tan messenger bag by the couch, pulled out two pill bottles, and handed them to Virginia. "One each." She watched as Virginia shook a pill out of each bottle, tossed them in her mouth and drank her grape juice. Taking the bottles back, Natalie returned them to the messenger bag.

Jordan watched them with interest, then said to Natalie, "You give her the medications?"

"Yeah. The oblong one is a strong opioid, and the other one is for inflammation. She can't remember time between pills very well. Last thing we need is her high on narcotics or accidentally overdosing."

"I see." He leaned forward and looked at Virginia. "You okay now?"

"I will be shortly. Now for our plan."

Jordan sat back. "Okay."

Virginia gave him a brief update on what they learned but left out the part about shooting the RPG on the reservation.

Jordan sat stoically. "Wow, you two have been busy. Well, the sheriff and I have suspected the owner of this retreat, Ellen Croft, as a possible suspect. Her father is a notorious… gangster in the region."

Natalie wet her lips. "We investigated him as well. He's retired and physically not in shape. He could mastermind this, but it's hard to think of some guy in his nineties doing it. However, Ellen Croft and her father are still on our radar. We believe she's working with someone else who's calling the shots, so why not daddy? She also knows about the quilt."

Jordan tilted his head. "Quilt? What quilt?"

Virginia shook her head. "I forgot about that. You tell him, Natalie."

Natalie gave him a description of the quilt and what they learned from it. "So, all that, plus what we learned from the tomahawk and the rock Virginia discovered with her now-broken foot, and what Terry told us, we know approximately where the gold coins are located."

"Okay, okay." Jordan shifted to the edge of his chair and leaned forward. "Where?"

Natalie stood and went to the railing of the stone scenic spot and pointed. "In the old lighthouse."

"That's impossible. People have rummaged through that old structure for… over a hundred years and never found anything of intrinsic value."

"That's because they didn't know where to look."

"One more question. Who is this Terry person you mentioned?"

Virginia sat back. "Terry works for me at the museum. She's a Ph.D.

anthropologist and archeologist, and I trust her." Virginia eyed her watch. "I'm hungry, let's go get something to eat."

Jordan ran his hands through his hair. "You want to eat now? We haven't spelled out the actual plan yet."

"Troops move on their stomachs, Agent Jordan. I think better when I eat."

Natalie shrugged her shoulder. "Yep, we'd better feed her and soon. When her blood sugar gets low, well... she gets... anxious and dangerous. She also thinks better when she's fed. The two pills she's taking don't diminish her mood swings, and without her occasional piña colada , white wine, or food, well... right now she's well behaved. But we don't want to put off lunch for very long."

Virginia pouted. "You two do know I'm sitting right here."

"Yes." Natalie adjusted her blouse, "Just warning our new partner in crime about you."

After lunch at the Inn, Virginia slung her black backpack over her shoulders and hobbled down to the base of the old lighthouse on her crutches with Agent Jordan and Natalie. She stopped and sat on a rock outcropping. "Okay, we're well away from eavesdroppers. First, we need to sidetrack Jake Thompson and Jason Ragget, the two treasure-hunting guys who have taken a shine to Natalie."

"Somehow I knew I'd be the goat in this," grumbled Natalie.

"Your job is very important. Lead them astray and out of my way. I'm sure you can do that easily and extremely well. That way they don't get hurt."

"Or impede the search for the coins," added Natalie.

"Right." Virginia turned to Jordan. "Now we need to," she made air quotes, "provide 'special information' to Linda Longfellow."

"Huh? I thought we were protecting one of the good guys."

"No. It was for show. She's the relative of John and Victoria Longfellow. They're Senecas and were the original owners of the lighthouse quilt. Once she thinks she knows where the treasure is and that we're going for it, I'm sure she'll pass that along to the gang, and they'll materialize and try to either stop us or wait until we retrieve the coins, then try and take them from us."

Jordan stared at Virginia. "Rest of the gang?"

"Oh, yeah. They're involved in an organized attempt to find the treasure. We don't believe they're with Ellen though. I think they're acting on their own and with other Senecas and aren't killers. When the amateur archaeologist, James St. Claire was murdered, it was because he found something that gave him an idea where the gold coins were located. After all this time, it gave the other gang some hope to find the missing gold. The problem was someone went about obtaining the information the wrong way and killed James St. Claire before they got what they wanted. We want them to engage us now."

Jordan swallowed. "We have two… two organizations after it?"

"Yes. Maybe three if you count the two guys that have a crush on Natalie. But I don't think they're killers."

"So, the main gang, Ellen's people… they've killed already; you want them to try and do it again… to us?"

"That's the idea. Only we know they'll try something. St. Claire didn't."

Natalie eyed Agent Jordan. "Virginia, I have the feeling it would be better if our FBI friend here took care of Jake Thompson and Jason Ragget, and I worked with you. I'll bring my duffle bag."

Virginia stared out at the light glistening off the lake and slowly nodded. "I think you're right. Agent Jordan, you keep the boys occupied while we go get the gold."

"Wh… why?" He frowned, "What duffle bag?"

"Because we have worked together for a few years and we may have to do some off the books stuff, and this way you aren't party to it. You'll have plausible deniability. You and deputy Ferguson of the sheriff's office will still get full credit for the capture of the criminals."

Jordan frowned. "But you two did all the work."

"Let me put it this way. If the time ever comes that we need your help again, what better way to get cooperation than from friends?"

He took a breath. "You have a point. Okay, I'll think of something to tie up the men for a while. When do we start?"

Virginia nodded toward the Inn. "Linda Longfellow and Ellen Croft are on the outside deck watching us down here by the old lighthouse. We have already started."

Natalie chuckled. "Now the fun starts." She glanced at Virginia. "Remember, Washington said to try and keep the body count down."

Jordan looked confused, and asked, "TRY to keep the body count down? Washington asked you to do that? Really?"

"Yeah. We can try, but don't count on it," Virginia said.

Jordan held up his hand in front of the women. "Wait, I just remembered… you didn't tell me about Natalie's duffle bag. What's so special about it?"

Virginia gave him a hundred-watt smile. "Where do you think we got the *special* mini-RPG that was used on the reservation?"

CHAPTER 29

Linda Longfellow and Ellen Croft stood on the balcony of the Inn overlooking the lake and old lighthouse. Ellen leaned on the railing and said, "They're having a private pow-wow with the FBI agent. Think Virginia and Natalie have found anything?"

"I have a gut feeling that they have made some discoveries. Why else would they be talking to the FBI? It would behoove you to keep a close watch on them. I'd love to know what's in the duffle bag Ms. North keeps with her."

"Do you think they have clues in it?" Ellen asked.

"Maybe. Why else would she guard it so well? I wonder if they've kept notes?" Linda asked.

"When they were gone yesterday, I searched their suite. I didn't find any notes or correspondence. They must be keeping everything in their heads or on their persons."

"I think I'll alert my brother and sister and get their take. They were close to Virginia."

Virginia leaned closer to Jordan. "Can you get a wiretap on their phones?"

"Way ahead of you. We've been monitoring all calls from here."

"Even cellphones?"

"No." Jordan sighed. "That's harder to do."

"We've been a little busy." Natalie wet her lips. "I'll send you the report we have on their cellphone use and who called them and who they called. You can do the legwork and find any unusual or frequent calls. We haven't had time."

Jordan stammered, "You... you have that? How? You need a warrant."

Natalie grinned. "Ever hear of the NSA?"

"Yeah. But you still need—"

"They cordially supplied us with it." She looked down at Bob Cat who was rubbing against her leg. She bent down and petted him. "Bob, I hope you're not a spy, too."

"Okay. How'd you two pull that off?" Jordan eyed the cat. "He's cute. I take it he lives here."

"Yes. And to answer your question, I sent a friend who works there a couple pictures of me from one of my films and promised to see him whenever I go to Washington or Maryland."

Jordan fumed. "That's not legal. You could go to prison for that!"

Natalie glared at him. "Arrest me."

Jordan closed his eyes, shook his head, then looked at Virginia and Natalie. "Okay. I'll take the report that I don't know where it came from and analyze it. If I'm going to be part of this team, I need to support you two. But please don't break too many more laws."

Virginia nodded. "We'll try." She glanced up at the balcony. "Ellen and Linda seem to have lost interest or are reporting that we may have found something important. I bet we get a call from Victoria Longfellow or John soon."

"Probably. What's next?" Natalie asked.

"Jordan will look at the NSA report and hole up Jake Thompson and Jason Ragget. You and I will casually be overheard planning on recovering the gold. If they haven't called the others in the conspiracy, they will then."

Natalie picked up Bob Cat. "The game's afoot."

Jordan frowned. "Huh?"

Virginia sighed. "Haven't you ever read Sherlock Holmes?"

"Ah… no."

"It's from *The Adventure of the Abbey Grange*. He awakens Watson by saying, 'Come, Watson, come. The game is afoot.' You need to get the complete works and read them. You should enjoy them being a cop and all."

Jordan raised an eyebrow. "You know the exact story that saying comes from?"

"I'm a big fan of Sherlock."

"Okay, reading Sherlock Holmes is now on my to-do list. I'll get started on the cellphone information as soon as I get it from Agent North. And I'll distract Jake Thompson and Jason Ragget."

Virginia rose, holding her crutches and leaned on them. "Okay, let's get going. We'll meet daily with a status report or sooner if something develops."

Jordan headed down to the lake shore while Virginia and Natalie, with her heavy duffle bag, walked up the winding concrete path to the Inn.

"Have you met Agent Connie Hathaway yet?" Natalie asked.

"Who?" Virginia was too distracted by the pain in her foot to grasp

Natalie's question.

"Agent Connie Hathaway," Natalie repeated. "Linda's bodyguard that Agent Jordan arranged? I haven't met her, and I haven't seen anyone new staying close to Linda."

Virginia shook her head. "No, I haven't."

As they continued toward the Inn, Virginia mumbled, "I hate crutches. I hope this foot thing doesn't last long."

"Not to worry, I'm here to help," Natalie said.

"I know, but I feel defenseless."

"Want me to strap a rifle to your crutch?"

Virginia stopped. "How about a shotgun?"

"I can do that. But I'll need to make sure you don't blow off the bottom of the crutch when you fire it."

Virginia hung her head. "That won't work. If I fired it while standing on one crutch, the recoil would knock me off my feet. I'll stick with a pistol." She continued up the walkway.

"This thing is heavy." Natalie hiked the duffle bag strap higher on her shoulder. "Want to go out to eat tonight? Maybe a little change of scenery would do you good, and we'd see if someone followed us."

Virginia looked at her *Mickey Mouse* watch. "Yeah, it's about that time. Okay, but since I can't drive with my foot and the drugs I'm taking, will you please promise to keep the speed less than a fighter jet? Where are we going? I take it you have somewhere in mind."

"Yes. Marvin Mozzeroni's Pizza & Pasta. It's on Main Street in Webster. It isn't all that far."

"Okay, let's go. I'm up for a pasta dinner. We can let Ellen know where we're going… one way or another."

Natalie's cellphone rang. She yanked it out of her pocket and answered it, then disconnected. "Guess who that was?"

"Victoria Longfellow. I heard part of the conversation," Virginia said. "Mentioning where we were going for dinner was genius. She wanted to know if we learned anything new, right?"

"Yep, it's like you were psychic. Now that I told her we have some new clues and are going to try and locate the gold coins, things should heat up."

"Yes. Now we've planted hints of our finding more clues with the FBI and the Seneca. My money is on the two men who are treasure hunters and maybe another party." Virginia turned, leaned on her crutches, and stared at the lake. "Now the fun begins."

Natalie set her duffle bag down. "Remember, Washington wants us to keep the body count down."

"We can try."

CHAPTER 30

Natalie parked their car on Main Street in Webster, New York, grabbed the crutches from the rear seat, and helped Virginia out of the car. They slowly walked to the restaurant and secured a table near the windows looking out onto the sidewalk and street.

Virginia perused the menu and ordered the ravioli with meat sauce, a meatball, and iced tea. Natalie selected eggplant parmesan and a glass of red wine. After ordering, they sat back and observed the establishment and the customers.

"No one here is taking any interest in us. That's good," Virginia said.

"Yeah, but we were followed from the Inn."

Virginia frowned. "We were? How did I miss that?"

Natalie shrugged her shoulder. "Your drugs, maybe. They can dull your senses."

"Apparently. Where are our tails now?"

"Sitting in a blue Toyota down the street, spying on the restaurant. One of them has binoculars. Us sitting by the window was a good idea. They can spy on us while we eat. If we make them hungry enough, maybe they'll come in here to eat and watch us."

"That would be funny. I hope we make them very hungry." Virginia looked around the restaurant and smiled. "This is a nice place, and the aroma of the spices and sauces is great. I needed this. Coming here was a good idea. After dinner, let's take a scenic ride home."

"Okay. That'll be fun. We can make a couple stops on the way to keep our tail guessing about what we are up to."

After a delicious dinner, Natalie slowly drove out of town and onto a double lane country road lined by maple, ash, cottonwood, walnut, oak trees, and bushes. The blue Toyota tried to inconspicuously follow them. Natalie pulled into a gas station, and she went inside to purchase a couple candy bars and use the restroom. Virginia watched from the car. After returning, Natalie sped off.

Virginia watched behind them as the Toyota pulled into the gas station and stopped at the pump island nearest the road. "Unless they need gas, that's going to be a wasted stop for them."

"Maybe they want to know what I did inside," Natalie said. "They can find out my choice in candy bars." Natalie skillfully unwrapped a Hershey bar while steering. "Did you see who was in the Toyota?"

"No. The pumps were in the way."

Natalie increased her speed and roared around corners. She slowed for a right turn, then sped down a single lane road as Virginia held her seatbelt in a death grip. Virginia, wide-eyed, asked, "What are you doing?"

"Look behind us."

Virginia glanced behind at the black GM SUV and spotted a similar vehicle trying to catch them. "Okay, I'm tired of this cat and mouse crap. When you find a suitable place for us to end this, stop there."

"Okay. Can you reach my duffle bag in the back seat?"

Virginia twisted around. "Yeah. Got it."

"There are a couple electromagnetic pulse grenades in it. Grab one and I'll slow down a little to let them get closer."

"Okay. I'll lob the EMP out the window. But then, put the pedal to the medal after I toss it. We don't need them shutting down all our electronics and the car."

"Right. This way we don't need to get in a gun fight." Natalie slowed the car and a minute later Virginia activated the time delay and tossed the EMP out the window. "Fire in the hole—go girl!" Natalie's acceleration pushed Virginia back in her seat.

Virginia and Natalie watched as the speeding two SUVs gained on them, then they suddenly slowed to a stop as they passed the small black device on the side of the road.

Virginia smiled. "They can't even call the Auto Club. Poor babies."

Natalie checked her rear-view mirror and finished her candy bar. "Looks like we're still causing problems back there. Two more cars approached the area where you threw our toy and have stopped as well. I hope no one else comes around for the next three minutes."

"No mess and no evidence."

Natalie looked around. "I like the scenery. Maybe now we can enjoy our drive." She glanced at Virginia. "Pull out your phone and use the navigation app to see where we are, then we can figure out where to go. It's still light, so maybe a little sightseeing would be in order."

Special Agent Jordan's cellphone rang as he ate dinner with Jake Thompson and Jason Ragget. He pulled it from his pocket and answered. "Jordan." He listened as his fists tightened. "You're FBI agents. How did this happen?" After listening and growing more tense he said. "Call the office and get them to send help. And I want a full report by tomorrow morning." He disconnected and stared at the other two men. "My agents lost Virginia and Natalie, and we have no idea who else was also following them."

Jake Thompson set his fork down. "How did the FBI lose them? I thought you guys were good."

Jordan took a breath. "They must have used some sort of EMP device to shut down the cars and all their electronics. From what my agent said, other vehicles and phones were cooked as well. One of the agents didn't have his phone on so it escaped damage."

"Where would they get an EMP device? Aren't they atomic bombs?"

Jordan gave them an exasperated expression. "Where did they get such items?" He clenched his teeth. "I don't know. And there are such things that don't need an A-Bomb to generate the pulses. Washington did say they were devious and dangerous. I greatly underestimated them."

John and Victoria Longfellow sat in disbelief. The phone call they had just received had upset them. John paced the floor and ran his fingers through his hair. "Linda said they lost Natalie and Virginia? How? They know this area better than the women. And what was it they said about some mysterious traffic jam?"

Victoria sat slouched on her couch. "The message was garbled. But they said Virginia and Natalie are in the wind. Linda has no idea where they went or what they are doing." She looked up at John. "They said someone else was following Virginia and Natalie, too. They are stopped as well."

John stopped pacing. "Someone else is following them? Who?"

"I have no idea."

John stepped to the front window and looked out at the lawn. "You told Linda to come here, didn't you? Virginia and her friend ended the pursuers following them, now they'll probably meander around to be safe, then also come to see us."

CHAPTER 31

Natalie pulled up into the driveway of Victoria Longfellow's home in Irondequoit and turned off the engine. "Well, we're here. I don't see anything suspicious around, do you?"

Virginia shook her head. "Just our SCSS agents watching the house. No FBI or anyone else. I think we can safely go inside." She opened the door, grabbed her backpack, slipped it on, pulled out her crutches, then hobbled toward the front steps.

Natalie grabbed her backpack and duffle bag, locked the car, and followed Virginia.

As they approached the front stoop, the door opened, and John stood there wide-eyed. "What happened to you?"

Virginia shook her head. "Broke my ankle."

"That's not good. Let me help you." He stepped outside and down the two steps, then helped Virginia climb the stairs. Once she was on the top of the stoop, he turned to Natalie. "Do you need help with that bag? It looks heavy."

"It's heavy, but I'm fine. Just get Virginia inside," replied Natalie.

Once they were in the living room, Victoria asked, "Why the sudden meeting? Linda called and said you contacted her and that it has something to do with the old gold coins. Did you find them?"

Virginia rested her ankle boot on a crutch to keep it elevated. "In a way. We know about where they are and how to locate them, but we have competition. We want your help. Linda agreed to be of assistance and said you two would help, too. So, we asked for a meeting of all of us to discuss how to proceed."

Victoria leaned forward. "You said there is competition. Who are they, and are they the killers of the amateur archaeologist? They're after the coins, too?"

"Yes, we have competition. Jake Thompson and Jason Ragget are after the gold coins, too. The archaeologist was on the trail of the coins when he was killed. We think they, and others, accidentally killed him before he could divulge any information."

"Where are they now?"

"FBI Special Agent Jordan is keeping an eye on them at the Inn, but he doesn't know that they are the murderers."

"We hope," muttered Natalie. "Don't forget the others who are involved."

"Others?" Victoria asked.

"Ellen Croft, her father, Graham Weedon, and her associates. She could be attached to Jake Thompson's and Jason Ragget's operation. We're still considering that aspect."

John jumped to his feet and peered out the front window. "Linda is here. Now we can get started."

John let Linda inside. When Virginia saw her, she asked, "Where's Agent Connie Hathaway?"

Linda looked confused. Then she said, "My bodyguard? I gave her the slip back at the Inn. I didn't think she needed to know we were meeting."

Victoria nodded and glanced at Natalie, who was keeping her face unreadable.

Linda sat on a blue overstuffed chair near the fireplace. "Virginia, I was glad to get your call. We, my siblings and I, want to help all we can."

Virginia climbed to her feet and leaned on her crutches. "Okay, we're all here. Natalie and I think we know where, or about where, the gold coins are. We need your help in actually finding them. But before we go any farther, we need to inform you that the killers will try to do two things. First, is to take the treasure from you, and second, they'll want to kill us because we know who they are. Our plan is to locate the treasure and have the killers come to us."

Victoria frowned. "Wait! That's dangerous!"

Virginia nodded. "Yes. We know who the killers are, but we need to catch them with the evidence." She returned to her seat and propped up her foot.

"How do we do that?" Linda asked.

Natalie pushed a stray hair from her face. "We have a plan. Here's what we're going to do."

CHAPTER 32

Virginia hobbled on her crutches down the dirt path from the Inn to the old lighthouse. Natalie walked behind Virginia with Linda beside her. They walked around rocks to the lakeside and along the lighthouse's massive stonework at the base.

Agent Connie Hathaway was nowhere to be seen, and Linda didn't mention her. Virginia decided not to bring up the subject again, but she was curious why neither she nor Natalie had seen or met her yet.

Virginia stopped and sat on a boulder. A light breeze off the lake ruffled her blonde ponytail. "I can't go any farther on these crutches. I'll just use the boot to walk."

"Oh, no you don't." Natalie's eyes narrowed. "I know you're the leader and usually in the fight, but I'm not letting you further hurt your ankle. It's broken and needs to heal. So, no walking along this trail without your crutches. It's treacherous enough with two good feet."

Linda nodded. "I agree with Agent North."

Virginia sighed with a dejected expression. "Okay, okay, I'm outnumbered. Go ahead and see if you can find the symbol of *Dagwanoeient,* the flying head spirit, and maybe the treasure." She rested her foot on the crutches. "I'll wait here and keep an eye out for any interlopers."

Natalie pointed. "You might want to move over there behind that stone alcove. It'll give you a better vantage point to see anyone coming and provide cover if you need it."

Virginia nodded. "Excellent idea." She limped to the alcove and sat behind a fallen stone block.

Natalie sat next to Virginia. "Okay. Keep an eye out for trouble. Oh, one more thing."

"What? Use sunscreen?"

"No. It's not a bad idea, though. You have your two-way radio in your backpack. I have its mate, so turn it on so we can communicate."

"Okay. Now go find *Dagwanoeient.*"

Natalie returned to Linda, and the two women started down the path.

Virginia adjusted her position so she could see the lake and the land approach from the side of the lighthouse. "Now we wait," she mumbled to herself. She found the walkie-talkie, turned it on, set it next to her, leaned back against a stone, and watched the others move on toward the shore entrance to the lighthouse. Virginia rubbed her forehead. *Why would someone build an entrance to the lighthouse at the bottom, facing the lake? Seems strange, but I don't design lighthouses.*

After about fifteen minutes, Virginia's radio crackled. She heard Natalie's excited voice. "We found a carving of *Dagwanoeient,* the flying head spirit. There is another symbol with it. Linda said it means something about going below."

"Going below where? You're on the lowest level now, aren't you?" replied Virginia.

"We looked around and found an opening hidden behind a cupboard and steps down. I'll contact you as soon as we find something."

"An opening? Like a secret passage? How'd you... never mind, good luck, and keep me posted."

Virginia rested against a stone and watched the lake and the path. She munched on crispy Chinese noodles from her backpack for what seemed like forever before she heard the far-off sounds of a motorboat well out in the lake. Pulling herself up, she shifted to a spot between two stone blocks and peered through the gap with binoculars from her backpack. The dark spot on the sunlit, smooth surface of Lake Ontario slowly turned toward shore. She grabbed the walkie-talkie and pressed the com button. "Natalie, we've got company coming by boat."

Natalie quickly responded. "How many are in the boat?"

"Can't tell exactly, three maybe, but I'm coming down there to you and Linda."

"Virginia! Your foot is—"

"On my way." Virginia put the radio back into her backpack, slipped it on, and climbed to her feet. Holding onto a boulder, she took one crutch. Using it to help support her, she hobbled down the uneven, slippery dirt path to the broken wooden lighthouse door hanging on one hinge. She carefully stepped over the threshold and entered the dank, cobweb filled and littered space. She glanced around, then jumped when she heard her name called from somewhere in the back of the stone-block walled room. Linda popped out of some obscure opening.

Linda motioned. "Virginia, this way."

Virginia limped to Linda and studied the section of wall where the women had torn away a faded-green stained, knotty-pine cupboard.

Linda pointed up toward a stone with some of the moss on it scraped away. *Dagwanoeient* and some other figures were barely visible.

Virginia nodded. "Glad you saw that."

"It was Natalie who found it. When I commented on her keen eye-sight, Natalie said she learned to spot these types of things from you."

Virginia slowly followed her through the opening and into a secret tunnel, yanked part of the cupboard back into place, and then went down a worn set of stone steps.

"Follow me, but be careful, some of the footing is wet, moss covered, and treacherous." As they started down the damp tunnel, Linda called over her shoulder, "While you were on lookout, we found something down here."

"You did? What?"

A motorboat slowly approached the rocky shore. After another ten minutes, the boat closed in on the beach, then ran up onto the wet sand near an old wooden dilapidated pier. The motor stopped.

Jake Thompson stepped out of the boat into about six inches of water. "Nuts," he mumbled. "There go the shoes." He, Jason Ragget, and another man hopped out of the boat and pulled it farther up onto the sand. Then they tied it to a small clump of trees.

Jake turned slightly and glanced up at the path. "Why didn't we just walk down here?"

The man with them turned. "The women came that way. They might have been watching for anyone following."

Jason shook his head slightly. "They probably know we're following them anyway. Why the rush to get close now? According to Agent Jordan, they said they were close to finding another clue, not the treasure."

"Ellen Croft said to take what he says with a grain of salt. By the time we get back, I'm sure she'll have persuaded him to give her more information." The man looked out into the lake. "Coming here by water was easier, and we weren't spotted."

Jake looked down at his wet shoes. "Easier? You do know that holding an FBI agent against his or her will is a federal felony."

The man chuckled. "So is murder on an Indian Reservation."

"Hey man, we didn't have anything to do with that."

"The cops won't buy it. You're now part of the whole thing. In for an inch, in for a mile."

Jason swallowed. His palms got clammy. He started to say something, then stopped, knelt and inspected the dirt path. "Looks like the ladies went this way and into the lighthouse."

The man walked to Jason and looked over his shoulder. "I agree. But why did they come here? Everyone has searched this place since the 1920s."

Jake shook his head. "I don't know. Maybe they found something everyone else missed."

"Well, we better get busy, those clouds across the lake are building and beckon a blow," the man said. "This may not be the best place to be in about a couple hours. You don't want to be on or near the lake during a big storm, or even a small one."

CHAPTER 33

Virginia followed Linda down the steps into a dark, narrow tunnel.

Linda stopped, and aimed the light down the passage. "This was made by people, it's not natural." She waved her light across visible cut marks. "See? It's hand cut."

"You're right." Virginia ran her free hand over the stone and wood walls as she hobbled next to Linda and focused her flashlight ahead. "It's chilly in here."

"Yeah. It's a bit brisk." Linda waved her light over the floor. "Watch your step, there are stones, and it's uneven."

The damp passageway went straight for about forty yards through spider webs and dust before coming to a stone, block-wall cavern about a hundred feet across. The opening contained a broken wooden table, an old, rusted metal folding chair, two shovels, a ladder, empty beer cans, and some paper trash.

Entering the space, Virginia said, "It smells somewhat musty in here." She wiped a cobweb off the low, stone-arched ceiling. "The walls aren't as cold as I would expect." Virginia turned and spotted Natalie on the far side of the space.

Natalie waved her light around. "Spiders. I don't like bugs, especially spiders. I hate them more than mayonnaise and salmon." She turned slightly. "I really hate mayonnaise and salmon."

Virginia nodded. "I understand. Leo, my cat, doesn't like salmon. I don't like mayonnaise and salmon either."

Natalie shone her light toward the ceiling. "Look. There are lights. I wonder if they still work?"

"If we can find the switch to turn them on, we can find out. It'll be easier to get around, especially if there are bugs waiting for us. But they may not be connected to their original power source anymore." Virginia swung her light around the walls. "If there's a light switch, it'll be near the entrance where we came in. Since we weren't looking for one, we might have passed it. Let's see what's in here." She found the switch and turned it on. The overhead string of lights came on and dimly lit the room.

Linda stood looking at the wires for the lights hung from the ceiling and the power switch. "Look at these wires. They seem to have cloth insulation and I'm not sure how well they've held up. Is using them safe?"

Virginia smiled. "Well so far, they haven't shorted out, so I guess using them will be okay. They used this type of wire in the early 1900s and close to the end of World War II." She stared at the lights for a moment. "I'm surprised they came on at all. I wonder if the power is from the Inn."

"Virginia!" Natalie called. "There's a crate over there." She waved toward the back of the cavern.

Virginia limped around the broken table covered with dust to the sturdy old wooden crate, and leaning on her crutch, she pulled the top off the crate. She peered inside. It was empty, save for a single gold coin. "There's one gold coin in here." Before she could reach for it, she heard Linda's hysterical voice.

"Som... someone is coming. If it's the men from the boat, we could be in trouble."

Virginia looked around. "If it's them in the tunnel already, then they've seen the light."

Natalie stepped behind the crate and examined the stone walls. She pointed at a smooth square rock sticking out slightly from the rest. Faintly visible was the figure of *Dagwanoeient* carved into it. "If you look closely, that stone looks different from the others. It's got that dreadful looking Seneca god figure on it."

Virginia bent forward for a closer look at the stone. "Yep, you're right. You've got good eyesight; I'd have missed this." She pushed on the stone. It moved slightly inward with a cracking sound. A section of wall creaked; it swung inward as it opened.

CHAPTER 34

Hearing footfalls in the tunnel, Virginia limped into the opening, followed by Linda and Natalie. After they had entered the space, Natalie pushed the massive stone door closed, followed by a resounding click.

Linda switched on her flashlight and swung it around. "I hope we can get out of here."

Virginia used her light to illuminate the area around the door. "Looks like another rock key like on the other side."

Linda and Virginia turned when Natalie called to them. "Look what I found. Another body, well… skeleton anyway. His skull doesn't look too good."

Virginia hobbled to Natalie, knelt, and examined the bones. "His head was bashed in by a heavy object."

Natalie frowned. "How long do you think he's been here?"

Virginia rummaged through the scraps of fabric around the body, then stood. "I'd guess about a century."

Linda stepped closer and looked at the disarticulated bones. "How do you know it's male and that it's been here for a hundred years?"

Virginia pointed at the remains. "The pelvis for one, and the skull. The clothes around him, as you can see, are decaying. They date from the early 1900s, and that newspaper next to what's left of his shirt has a faint date on it. The year is 1923. Then there's that rusting .38 caliber police special revolver over there."

Natalie moved a section of the pants the man had worn when a gold coin fell out onto the floor. "I bet he was the guy who stole the treasure from the original thieves. But where is the treasure, and who bashed his head in?"

"We'll never know who exactly killed him. But I bet it was a Seneca who did it."

Linda stiffened. "How the hell do you know that?"

"He was clubbed to death. You can tell by the shape of the wound in the skull and the broken ribs and his wrist. And… the club was a stone tomahawk." Virginia pointed with her light. "It's sitting over there near that hollow spot in the back stone wall. It's Seneca."

Linda hurried across the dirt floor to the weapon and peered down at it. "You could be right."

"Bring it over here, and let's see if it fits the head wound."

Linda bent down and picked up the tomahawk. She examined it, then stepped to Virginia and handed it to her.

Virginia took the weapon, and sitting on the dirt floor, tried to fit the stone head of the tomahawk with the skull wound. "It sort-of-fits. A pathologist will need to make sure." She glanced up at Natalie by the entrance they came through. "What are you doing?"

"The men on the other side have found the box and are now searching for what happened to us. With our luck, they'll stumble on the key stone. There must be another way out."

"There is. It's the way the people who killed this man left after re-hiding the treasure."

Linda eyed Virginia. "You know where it is? How?"

Virginia shined her flashlight toward the right side of the cavern. "Because they hid the treasure again and left that way."

Linda waved the beam of her light around. "I don't see it." She looked at the earthen floor. "No signs of digging or footprints except ours. So, where is the treasure? They must have taken it."

Natalie hurried to the far side of the chamber, where Virginia's light was shining. "There's nothing but stone here." She put her hand on a boulder, then frowned. "That's odd." She bent forward and examined it. "That's a man-made rock." She swung around aiming her light at the walls. "Here's another tunnel entrance around this corner. There's a slight breeze from it. It's well hidden... and it's narrow."

Linda rushed to Natalie and felt the fake rock. "This looks like something from Disneyland. It really looks like a big rock. Why's it here?"

"Because the treasure is hidden under it," Virginia said. "And note that there are no boulders like that in here or outside. It had to be the hiding place."

Natalie moved her head back and forth, examining the artificial boulder. "The treasure is under here, really?" She pushed on the artificial boulder. "It's heavy."

Virginia nodded. "Yes. The treasure is there. It has to be heavy so as not to move easily and protect the gold coins."

"I never would have guessed," Linda added as she rested her hand on it. "Why would whoever killed that man just leave it hidden here? Why not take it out and use it?"

"Because every cop in New York State and Canada were looking for it. Those coins showing up suddenly would be suspicious. And they are tied to the murders of the original thieves. The guy stored them here until things cooled off but was pounced upon and killed by the Seneca back then."

Natalie returned to the portal they entered from and listened. "That's all good and stuff but the guys on the other side of the wall are looking for a secret compartment and may find the special rock soon. We'd better vamoose."

Linda stood in shock. "Wait, if they find the treasure, then all is lost. They'll just take it out in their boat, and we'll never find it."

"I know." Virginia smiled. "But why not let them do the heavy lifting for us."

Linda swallowed. "But—"

Natalie shook her head and grinned. "We let them get the gold coins on their boat, then bring the hammer down. And we catch the archeologist's killer in one fell swoop."

Virginia pointed at the new tunnel entrance. "Natalie, take Linda and go out. You know what to do when you get to the surface."

"Yes. What are you going to do?"

"Use the contents of your duffle bag to stall for time. I'll then follow you out."

CHAPTER 35

Virginia limped to the boulder, dragging Natalie's duffle bag with her, then she sat on the ground. She opened the bag and inspected the contents. *This'll be fun.* She removed the remaining EMP devices and activated them. She planted one near the entrance and another near the boulder and pocketed the activation switch. Then she removed a flash-bang grenade and set it up under the edge of the big rock. *This'll disorient them, cause a little pain, and slow them down, but won't destroy anything.* Next, she hobbled across the cavern, stretching a thin wire that was attached to a canister of bear-strength pepper spray with a small charge attached to blow the canister open and rapidly fill the room with the ingredients. She then removed the last of the contents, a short-barreled 12-gauge semiautomatic shotgun loaded with fifteen rounds and clipped it to her crutch. She switched on her flashlight, and with the shotgun-crutch combination, she wormed her way through the narrow, dark tunnel toward the surface.

After a few minutes of squeezing through the constricted, winding passage, she saw a light ahead. At the same time, Virginia heard the explosion from the cave and the screams of the men behind her. She smiled, pulled the EMP trigger box from her pocket and triggered it. *So much for all their digital equipment like cellphones. The flash-bang grenade will come in a few minutes. That, along with the pepper spray, will make their day.* She kept moving toward the light at the end of the tunnel. The tunnel roof sloped down as she neared the opening. Now crawling and pushing her crutch ahead of her, she heard voices. As she slowly moved forward, the cave end of the tunnel illuminated and the bang roared up the tunnel. Virginia froze for a moment. *There goes the grenade with a bright flash and bang. I won't need to worry about them for a while. I wonder if anyone outside heard that muffled sound.* She smiled to herself and inched on ahead.

At the end of the tunnel, she crawled behind the bushes blocking the small hole of the entrance from view. She carefully spread the branches and peered out and around a section of the lighthouse. She spotted Natalie and Linda sitting on a low stone wall. Standing in front of her was John, Victoria Longfellow, FBI Special Agent Jordan, and Ellen Croft with a semiautomatic pistol aimed at Natalie. *Doesn't look like they heard the flash-bang grenade go off.*

Ellen glanced around, then said, "Just exactly where did you come from? Last I heard you were underground somewhere."

Natalie just smiled.

Linda cleared her throat. "We were, but we got out just before your henchmen came after us."

"So, they're still down there looking for you?"

Natalie took a deep breath and slowly let it out. "They'll be trying to get out themselves but will probably need help."

Ellen's brow furrowed. "Why is that?"

"Because Virginia is still there, and that won't be good for them. They'll be lucky to get out without injury or even get out alive."

"There are three men down there against one woman who is crippled. Not much of a contest."

Natalie chuckled. "You're right about that. She'll make short work of them. You're next."

"I don't think so. She's on crutches. What can she do to them?" Ellen looked around nervously. "Nothing, that's what."

She tried using her walkie-talkie to reach the men in the cave. "Not getting a response." She shook her head. "Them being underground must have cut off the signal."

"That or they're dead," Natalie responded.

Ellen turned. "Agent Jordan, go take a look, but be careful."

Natalie looked at Agent Jordan and then at Linda. "Whatever happened to Agent Connie Hathaway?" she asked.

"Who?" Agent Jordan asked, smiling.

Natalie nodded. "Ahh... there was no bodyguard, was there? You didn't need any more feds poking around, getting in your way." Then she asked, "So, Mr. FBI Man, why are you siding with the criminals?"

Jordan shrugged his shoulder. "The gold coins will make a better retirement than my government pension."

"But there's been a murder."

"Yeah, shit happens." He turned to walk past John and Victoria when John stopped him.

John's eyes narrowed. "What do you mean shit happens? Are you responsible for the amateur archaeologist James St. Claire's murder?"

"No, Ellen killed him. That was tragic because whatever he found died with him. At least until Virginia and Natalie came on the case. But now we have the treasure, so Virginia and Natalie are excess baggage."

Natalie grinned. "But Virginia and I are expensive baggage, as you will soon discover."

John glared at Ellen. "James St. Claire was a good man. You murdered him in cold blood!"

"I didn't want to." Ellen rubbed her forehead. "He was stubborn, and the tomahawk was handy. I thought I'd threaten him, but things got out of hand."

John collapsed on the stone retaining wall. "I want no part in this. Victoria and I didn't sign up for any killing. We just wanted the treasure."

"Too late. You consulted on this, helped keep me apprised of Virginia's investigation, and now you helped capture Natalie and your siblings. You're as guilty as if you used the tomahawk yourself. Same with your sister, Victoria." Ellen waved her pistol. "Jordan, go see to the others below."

Natalie noticed the bushes near the hidden entrance move and smiled. "You know, Ellen, holding us at gunpoint and having a corrupt FBI agent working for you might not sit well with Virginia."

"Virginia won't be around long enough to worry about it, " Ellen sneered.

As Jordan started for the path, Virginia climbed out of the tunnel, leaned against the stone lighthouse, raised her crutch with the shotgun, and aimed at Ellen. "Stop where you are, Agent Jordan," she yelled, "and drop the gun, Ellen. You two put your hands up real high."

Ellen swung around with her pistol aiming at Virginia. The shotgun roared. Ellen stepped back a couple feet with wide eyes, dropped her gun, and grabbed her abdomen. She stood for a second, then slumped to the ground.

Jordan swung around, yanked his sidearm out from under his jacket and started to aim at Virginia when three shots rang out from a pistol in Natalie's hands. Jordan stumbled forward with a surprised expression, then fell to the ground.

Virginia watched John and Victoria over the barrel of her shotgun. "Don't move."

Victoria stammered. "Okay. But ca... can we put our hands down? We aren't armed and..."

"Yeah, but no sudden moves." Virginia glanced at Natalie who was examining Ellen and Jordan. "Where'd you get the gun?"

"Under my blouse in the back. Ellen is alive but barely. Jordan is dead. Looks like one of my bullets went through his arm, into his chest, and must have hit his heart." Natalie stood. "Now that the two biggest threats are down, do you want me to go see about the boys below?"

"No, I'll do that."

"You've got a broken foot."

"I know." Virginia looked up at the black clouds above as a cold breeze swept through. "I need you to call Tom at the Smithsonian Central Security Service and get a clean-up team, medics, and backup here ASAP.

Also, watch these two. That storm is about to hit, and it looks like it's going to be a beauty. Take John, Victoria, and Linda to the Inn if you want. And hand me Ellen's gun, will you please?"

Natalie frowned, picked up the pistol and handed it to Virginia. "More reason for me to go down there than you. I have two good feet." She stared at Virginia. "Okay, be hardheaded. I'll take care of things here, go round up the guys. But be careful."

Virginia smiled. "Aren't I always?"

"No," Natalie declared.

Virginia tucked the pistol into her belt under her shirt, then hobbled around the group and down a pea-gravel path when it started to rain. *Now it decides to rain. Just what I don't need.* She reached the bottom of the lighthouse and looked out at the lake. Three-foot waves were breaking on the shoreline. The lake looked gray and mad. Lightening ripped the black sky out across the lake. She stepped into a niche in the stone base of the lighthouse and watched the motorboat tied up along the shore, where Jake Thompson and Jason Ragget loaded bags of gold coins from two crates into the boat.

Jake stepped out of the water and arched his back. "Damn, those bags are heavy. I'm glad we used block and tackle to get the two boxes through the tunnel from the cavern below. Good thing the coins are in bags."

Jason nodded. "When that flash-bang thing went off it split that fake rock. Good thing it did, or we may never have found the coins. We would never have gotten the chest in the boat. It weighs over half a ton."

Virginia watched them rubbing their eyes and coughing. *They recovered from my toys faster than I thought they would. That bear spray should have blinded them for longer or done more damage. Must be old.*

Jason nodded as he glanced around. "Where's Brad?"

"I'm coming. Just wanted to make sure that Virginia dame isn't still in the cave or around here watching us," Brad said. "This rain is suboptimal."

"Suboptimal? What? Are you James Bond now?" asked Jake sarcastically.

"I was in the Marines Expeditionary Force," Brad responded.

Virginia frowned. *So that's the third man. He's got to be six feet six inches tall and built like a wrestler. Blond crew cut and all.* She shifted her attention to the boat. The stern was dangerously low in the water. *Those coins and the three of them will overload that boat. That's not good in calm weather. This storm will sink it.* She moved her crutch, causing a small rockslide of pebbles.

Brad spun around, pulling a pistol out of his belt. "What was that?"

"Probably just some small rocks moving in the wind and rain," Jason said.

"It came from up there," Brad said. "I'll check it out."

CHAPTER 36

Virginia restlessly shifted her weight in the narrow niche and watched the pebbles tumble down the dirt slope. *Shit, that's not good.* She looked around the edge of the stone lighthouse and saw Brad heading her way with his gun aimed at her hiding spot. *That's not good either. I wish I had my can of crispy Chinese noodles right about now. No lunch. This is nuts. A bad man is heading my way with a gun, and I want Chinese noodles? Think, Virginia.*

Brad stopped about ten feet downslope from Virginia and looked at the massive stone structure, then turned back toward the boat. "Looks like you were right, Jason, just some pebbles sliding down. Probably due to the wind." He turned and marched back to the boat and the other two men. "Okay, let's get this thing untied and get out of here."

Jake stood next to the boat. "Where are we going with it? The storm is getting stronger. I'm not sure we should take it out on the lake. Those waves have whitecaps, and the boat is low in the water."

"Yeah, look at those clouds," Jason said as lightning flashed from the clouds to the surface of the lake. Thunder roared.

Virginia slipped out of her hiding place into the now increasing rain and ambled toward the men as they gazed out at the lake. She stopped about twenty feet away from them, leaned against a dead tree stump, and raised her crutch, aiming the shotgun at them. "Okay boys, raise your hands."

Jason and Jake spun around. Seeing Virginia with her crutch raised, they started to laugh. Jason said, "You going to shoot us with a crutch? This isn't third grade."

"Where did you come from?" Brad demanded.

Virginia fired a shot that ripped part of the gunnel off the bow of the boat. "No. The crutch is for support, Bozo. And I move in mysterious ways."

Jake and Jason slowly raised their hands. Brad did likewise.

Virginia trudged through the mud and forming puddles along the path toward the men. She realized with one crutch the going was getting tough, and the same crutch she was using for support also held her shotgun. She limped along when suddenly, she saw Brad drop his hands, yank his pistol from his belt, and aim it at her.

"Don't even think of raising that crutch, Honey," Brad said. "Just continue this way."

"No one calls me honey but my husband," Virginia stated firmly.

"Now ain't that sweet? Your husband is going to be a widower shortly, *Honey.*"

Virginia fumed as she lumbered to the boat and stopped in front of the bow and the line holding it in place. Her broken foot throbbed. "Jake asked you a question, Brad. Where do you think you're going with the boat overloaded like this?"

Brad surveyed the lake. "It has to stay afloat just long enough to get us a couple miles east of here. I have a cabin in a sheltered cove there. That's where we'll unload the chest and divide the spoils of our adventure."

"How about Ellen? You going to count out her share or cut her out of the deal, like you're going to cut these two guys out?" Virginia looked at Jake and Jason, then back at Brad. "Tell you what, since I'm not going to get any of the coins, I'll just stay here," Virginia said.

Brad gave her a sinister grin. "No, you're going with us out about a mile or so, then you'll go swimming. With that funny boot on your foot, the cold water, and the waves, you'll just become a casualty of the lake." He waved his gun at her. "Drop the crutch and climb into the boat."

"Wait," said Jake. "What does she mean cut us out?"

Virginia shrugged her shoulder. "Ellen killed the archaeologist. She's in cahoots with the FBI agent on this caper. She hired Brad. But you heard him. *He* has the cabin in a secluded cove, not her. What makes you think he's going to split millions of dollars with you and her? You are now extra weight that can be cut loose."

"Shut up and get in the damn boat," yelled Brad. Thunder roared, and the sky turned inky. He waved his gun at them. "You two, help her get in. Time's running out. The storm is getting worse."

Virginia dropped her crutch and limped to the side of the boat. The pain in her foot worsened. She tried to lift herself up without much success. She twisted around. "Give me a hand will you, Jake?"

Jake took Virginia's arm and steadied her, and she rolled into the boat, her massive boot slamming against the side as she tumbled.

Virginia screamed from the pain that shot through her from her broken foot. Jake and Jason climbed in and helped her up and to a seat in the middle of the boat. They took seats in front and faced her. She smiled at them and received confused looks in return.

Then, after Brad untied the boat and hopped in, he maneuvered around everyone to the stern and started the massive Mercury one-hundred-and-fifty horsepower outboard motor. He backed the boat up, then turned into the increasingly larger waves and gently pushed the throttle to gain momentum. The overloaded boat pushed through the waves, taking on water with each one.

Virginia examined the boat. *Couldn't he have gotten a bigger one? This is not much more than a twenty-foot rowboat.* She turned in her seat and watched Brad steer the boat out into the lake, driving it through and over the cresting waves and whitecaps. Water splashed into the boat from each wave the boat powered through. *The rate this tub is taking on water, we won't get very far.* Her wet clothes clung to her. She felt her wet matted hair. Virginia slowly undid the fasteners on her boot.

Brad yelled over the wind, rain, and the sound of the outboard motor. "I'll take us out about a mile or two then lighten the load. Virginia, you'll go overboard first."

Jake's eyes widened. "What do you mean she goes *first?*"

"You didn't really expect me to share this treasure with you, did you?"

Virginia looked back at the old lighthouse and saw Natalie standing on the shore with a two-way radio to her ear.

CHAPTER 37

Jake and Jason turned pale at what Brad said. Jake leaned slightly forward toward Virginia and whispered, "Any ideas on how to get out of this alive? Will you help us?"

Virginia just smiled, then said, "Just sit there and don't get in my way or I'll toss you two into the lake."

Jake nodded. "Okay."

Virginia turned in her seat and looked at Brad. His pistol was tucked in his belt in the front. She watched his concentration on the increasingly enlarging waves and trying to make careful adjustments to direction and speed as more water poured into the boat. Virginia quickly reached behind her and under her wet blouse, yanked out her pistol and aimed it at Brad. "Don't reach for your gun or I'll blow a big hole in you. Now carefully turn us around and head for shore."

Brad fumed. His face distorted with rage, and he growled, "I should have shot you on shore. Now I'll just dump you out here." He reached for his gun when Virginia pulled the trigger of her gun three times. The first two bullets struck Brad in the chest, the third went through his neck. He sat and didn't move as his gun fell from his limp hand. Then he reached for his throat and started to stand when a wave slammed with jarring force into the boat from the front right side, knocking him over the stern and into the lake. The motor hesitated for a second as the propeller sliced through part of his leg.

Virginia rose slightly and inched toward the stern, her foot throbbing. She took ahold of the control arm of the outboard motor, when it sputtered and died. She shook her head. "Shit. Not what I need now. Why did he draw his weapon when I had the drop on him?" She leaned close to the motor housing and noticed a round bullet hole in the engine compartment. "I killed Brad and the motor." She sighed. "Good job, Virginia." She grabbed the side of the boat as it floundered in the waves.

Jake looked at her with wide eyes. "You... you killed him."

"Yeah, how about that? And I killed the motor, so unless you want to swim, we'd better figure out how we're going to keep this tub afloat. We can't even steer. These waves will sink us in short order."

"What? How? I mean, what are we going to do?" Jason asked holding the side of the rocking boat.

Virginia looked toward the almost invisible shore through the downpour. "The coast is about half a mile or maybe a little more away. Can you swim?"

"Not that well, and the water is cold and rough." Jason's voice increased in pitch. "We're going to drown."

Virginia examined the floundering boat. It was dangerously low in the water. Then she froze and listened. Through the thundering wind, she heard a faint thump… thump… thump coming from the west. "I hope that's what I think it is," she said to herself. Virginia looked toward the sound as it steadily increased in volume. Then out of the low, dense, inky clouds, a helicopter lowered over them.

A voice came over a speaker. "Virginia Clark. This is the U.S. Coast Guard. We are lowering a diver with a harness down to you. He will assist in getting you out of there."

Virginia's heart raced. "My heroes, yet again." She watched as a man in a dark wetsuit was lowered down. When he landed on the boat, he spoke to Virginia. "I'll fasten you into this harness and they will pull both of us up to the chopper. Okay?"

She nodded. "Whatever you want to do is fine with me." She stood close to the diver and let him fasten the harness around her.

Jake stood rocking the boat more. "Hey, how about us?"

The diver looked at Jake and Jason, then back at Virginia and winked. "What do you want to do with them?"

Virginia squinted at them, then said, "I'd let them swim, but I guess we should try and get them off this thing, too."

The diver nodded at the men. "Once we get Virginia on the chopper, we'll come back for you, assuming this thing stays afloat that long." He waved his arm. The cable went taught. Virginia and the diver were lifted as one to the waiting helicopter, like a rag doll swaying in the wind.

After being pulled into the rocking chopper, Virginia took a seat on the opposite wall from the door. A coastguardsman gave her a blanket that she wrapped around herself. She sat shivering as the diver brought Jake and Jason on board. They sat away from Virginia and were not offered blankets. The helicopter hovered for another minute, then rose.

The copilot stepped into the rear cabin, knelt, and handed Virginia a map. "Agent Clark, we marked on the chart exactly where your little boat went down. Maybe you can recover what was in that box when the weather clears."

Virginia looked at his rank insignia as she took the map. "Thank you,

Lieutenant. I take it the thing sunk."

He laughed. "Oh, yeah. There was no way that thing was going to stay afloat in those waves."

"May I ask where you're going to take us?"

"Strong Memorial Hospital ER in Rochester. We were told to stay with you to help guard these prisoners until your agency arrives."

"How did you know we were in trouble, sir?" Virginia asked.

"Your partner got ahold of someone who got ahold of someone else and all of a sudden we were ordered to come and get you by our district admiral. He said if we lost you not to come back. Someone pretty high up in the food chain seems to like you."

Virginia closed her eyes and smiled. "Natalie. Well, Lieutenant, thank you for saving us. You guys are the unsung heroes of our country and especially my heroes."

"Thank you." He smiled, then handed Virginia a headset and plugged it into a socket. "You can use this to listen in on our conversations and talk to us." He stood up and walked back to the cockpit.

Virginia settled back, put on the earphones, and listened. She heard the pilot call the hospital. "Coast Guard Rescue Six to SMH Emergency, we are inbound, ETA seven minutes. Three for evaluation that we plucked out of Lake Ontario. One female and two males. Subjects conscious but showing signs of hypothermia."

"Rescue six, this is Strong Emergency, do you have paramedics on board?"

"Negative."

"Roger. Use Hilo pad four on arrival."

"Roger, Hilo pad four. Oh, have federal officers arrived?"

"No. Why would they?"

"We have a federal agent on board with two suspects and her agency is sending backup. We will remain with them until her backup arrives."

"This is— Wait, an agent is here now. She's quite concerned about her partner."

"Tell her that Agent Clark is fine, but cold."

"Okay. Strong Emergency out."

Virginia smiled. *I like these coast guard guys. They know how to take care of a lady.*

In the hospital emergency examining room, Virginia put dry clothes on that Natalie had brought for her. She took her crutches that Natalie had retrieved from the cave and beach and hobbled, with Natalie carrying a bag with Virginia's wet clothes, to the waiting area. She watched as three U.S. Marshals and Deputy Ferguson took Jason and Jake in handcuffs out to a waiting van. Virginia shook her head. "They only wanted the treasure. They had nothing to do with the murder of the archaeologist." They followed the marshals out into the parking lot. "It stopped raining."

"I know, " Natalie said. "But they were with that other guy who you said was going to cheat Ellen and them out of the treasure and when we shot her and killed the FBI agent, they got caught up in it just like Victoria and John."

"We need to see what we can do for them. They were not party to the ploy."

"Already started to do that."

Virginia stopped in the middle of the parking lot. "What do you mean?"

"I talked to our boss in Washington and told him what was going on and who was who in the zoo. The Smithsonian Central Security Service is waiting for our field reports and will get with the U.S. Attorney about charges, or lack thereof. But Ellen, if she survives, is going to stand trial for murder on the Seneca Indian Reservation, conspiracy to commit murder, and attempted murder of a federal agent."

"You did all this while I was out on that boat and getting airlifted to here?" Virginia asked. "And you even beat me here."

"I was concerned about you," Natalie said. "And I got Deputy Ferguson of the Monroe County Sheriff's Office to take Victoria and John to jail to hold them until we decide what to do with them. They are just being detained and aren't arrested… yet. The deputies came with the paramedics to get Ellen. Deputy Ferguson came, too. There are SCSS agents at the hospital guarding her."

"That, my dear, was fast. How did you get here before me?"

"I used my charms on a young deputy who escorted me here with lights and sirens."

"Well, I'm really glad to see you. For a while there, it was touch and go. And I'll tell you one thing, being out on Lake Ontario in a storm is not for the faint of heart."

"Well, we got that case wrapped up."

"Not so fast. I need to call Tom in Washington." Virginia fumbled for her phone in her backpack.

"Why?"

"I found out who was masterminding all this."

"Who?"

"Ellen's father, Graham Weedon. He may be in his nineties but he's still sharp. He's wanted the treasure since he first heard of it after World War II. I found his number on Ellen's phone."

"He's her father. Of course he's on her phone," stated Natalie.

"Yes, but there are some voicemails instructing her on what to do."

"When did you have time to do all that?"

"In the chopper on the way here to the hospital. I stole her phone before I went to find the chest with the coins and the guys and went for a boat ride. It's kind of funny that he was going to have the others all killed so he and Ellen could go away and enjoy life someplace with nice weather and no extradition."

"Call Tom." Natalie helped Virginia into the car. "I think we should go to dinner. I'm hungry."

"You're always hungry."

"Yeah, but you're going to need to eat and get your strength up."

"Why?"

Natalie gave Virginia a sheepish grin as she exited the parking lot. "You need to talk to your husband."

"What! Did you call Andy? You didn't need to upset him."

"I had to tell him you were being flown to the hospital by the coast guard after being rescued from a boat that was sinking on Lake Ontario in a storm. I didn't know about the shootout with an outboard motor at the time, though."

Virginia slumped in her seat. "Thanks a heap."

"No problem. Want Italian for dinner with a little wine?"

"Italian is a food group, and make it a lot of wine. I'll take the pain meds for my foot later. Then let's call Deputy Ferguson at the sheriff's office and get Victoria and John released. We'll return the lighthouse quilt to them just before we leave to go home. Then we can have the marshals release Jake and Jason. They all got in over their heads but are not criminals."

Natalie headed toward the restaurant she had selected ahead of time. "What about the treasure?"

"It's now at the bottom of Lake Ontario. But the coast guard gave me a map showing exactly where the boat went down. So tomorrow, assuming this storm passes by then, we can arrange to retrieve it."

"Who will get the gold coins?" Natalie asked.

"I don't know. I'll bet all sorts of people, government agencies, and even the Seneca Nation will file claims. But until the courts sort it out, the Smithsonian will hold the treasure." Virginia pointed out the window. "Is that the restaurant?"

"Yep."

"Nice choice. Park while I call Tom. Then we can go for the wine. I'm going to need it."

ABOUT THE AUTHOR

Dr. David Ciambrone is a retired aerospace and defense company executive, scientist, professor of engineering, and a business and environmental consultant and is now a best-selling, award-winning author, living in Georgetown, Texas. He has published twenty-six (26) books: four (4) non-fiction, two (2) textbooks for a California university, and twenty (20) mysteries. He is the author of the Virginia Davies Quilt Mysteries.

Dave has been a speaker at writer's groups, schools, colleges, libraries, quilt guilds, writer's conferences, and business/scientific conferences internationally.

Dr. Ciambrone also wrote three newspaper columns and wrote a column for a business journal.

Dave is a member of Sisters in Crime, the San Gabriel Writer's League, the Writer's League of Texas, Mystery Writers of America, the International Thriller Writers Association, The Beacon Society, and DFW Sherlock Holmes Society.

Dave was appointed a U.S. Treasury Commissioner and to the management board of the Resolution Trust Corporation (RTC) by President Clinton.

He is a Fellow of the International Oceanographic Foundation.

Visit David at

Author's Website:davidciambrone.com

Facebook:facebook.com/david.ciambrone?fref=ts

Twitter:twitter.com/mysterywriter5

LinkedIn:linkedin.com/pub/david-ciambrone-sc-d-fiof/11/ab5/bb3

Amazon:amazon.com/author/davidciambrone

Progressive Rising Phoenix Press is an independent publisher. We offer wholesale pricing and multiple binding options with no minimum purchases for schools, libraries, book clubs, and retail vendors. We offer substantial discounts on bulk orders and discounts on individual sales through our online store. Please visit our website at:

www.ProgressiveRisingPhoenix.com

If you enjoyed reading this book, please review it on Amazon,
B & N, or Goodreads.
Thank you in advance!

Milton Keynes UK
Ingram Content Group UK Ltd.
UKHW030142051224
452010UK00001B/213